GRACE
ABOUNDING

Maureen Howard

GRACE
ABOUNDING

Little, Brown and Company — Boston – Toronto

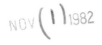

Second Printing

LIBRARY OF CONGRESS CATALOGING IN PUBLICATION DATA

Howard, Maureen, 1930–
    Grace abounding.

    I. Title.
PS3558.08823G7 1982   813'.54   82-14056
ISBN 0-316-37462-8

MV
Designed by Susan Windheim

Published simultaneously in Canada
by Little, Brown & Company (Canada) Limited

PRINTED IN THE UNITED STATES OF AMERICA

For Mark Probst

Do not despair; one of the thieves was saved.
Do not presume; one of the thieves was damned.

SAINT AUGUSTINE

ALSO BY MAUREEN HOWARD

SIN

MAUDE visits two old women — her mother, who is strong in body, dispirited in mind; the mother's nurse, who is ailing but spirited and bright. On alternate tracks the old women pace the room at night. Duty bound, Maude brings them their prescriptions. She knows what foods grow stale on their shelves. She knows the nurse drinks in the pantry. Her mother will not bathe. After each visit Maude escapes to the privacy of her car with an odd happiness: it may be undeserved euphoria or passionate relief. When Maude returns home she is bewildered each time, even saddened, by the neighbor house of two old sisters, a plant in their window, curtains and lamp of a life she cannot know or understand.

Now I am going home. The air in the front left tire is low. A familiar slow leak, all winter into spring. Driving the highways in late wet snow. Begging for a blowout in the slush. Any small accident going — scene with a state trooper, his bull-neck pocked white in the cold. Mud, drizzle, hubcaps and soda cans in the mild slope of a culvert, then the fast beat and flash of a tow truck's emergency light. My policeman takes me into the warmth of his patrol car, strokes, in routine fashion, the handle of his gun, then the knob of his erect shift. Slowly he shoves aside a book of traffic citations with his boot so that he may . . . and shuts off the babble of heart attacks, rapes, cat's in a tree, so that when he takes off his Stetson we may . . . A red welt scores his forehead as though he has been bearing the weight of a crown.

Scene of crude lust, a truck driver jacking me up. He lies in the black cinders of a soft shoulder. My shredded rubber and his goodwill. The little lady in distress going home; if the tire doesn't blow I am going; if there is not a scene to detain me as I turn off the interstate onto the back road, I am going home. But there, by the ramp, two boys in the high flush of youth are hitching a ride. Ripe, sweaty boys who have been kicking a soccer ball or running bases. Smelling of sour socks and apple cores they enter my life with their acne polished raw, and when they talk to me it is with cruel politeness. Bob and Tom for three miles. In a lonely grove by a trash can they inspect my low tire — Tom or Bob, bending to pick just a pebble out of the tread, shows an expanse of tender flesh down to the buttocks as his sweat shirt pulls up from his jeans. They are innocent, Bobby and Tom. Their conversation, dull and hesitant, is delivered in deep, untried voices. Squat Tom, whose braces will cut my lips as we kiss. Big Bob, who has not yet shaved the sparse stubble off his manly chin. After three miles I am discarded at a general store where they will buy Coke and cigarettes without me.

Going is like this — on the back roads, up through
Easton by the reservoir that has been gouged out of a
valley. Acres of brooding pine forest imported from
Maine by the Hydraulic Company, a placid false beauty,
and in the shadows I fancy a musty cabin, wet bathing
suits thrown on branches, the damp ticking of a bare
mattress where we lie with gooseflesh and blue shriveled
nipples after a chill swim — denying, as I drive by untroubled waters, the posted command that I never set foot
on their stage set of russet needles. On the back road I
pass mysterious antique shops that are never open, a dingy
country inn, ten real-estate shingles, a gun store where
one day as I am driving home I price (but do not buy) a
small silver pistol that fits neatly in my purse.

I am going home to a tall house that sits high on a bed
of granite, a white clapboard house with shutters of
handsome blood red, a house that can fill you with memories though you have never lived within. There is, of
course, a front porch with fat columns and lacy brack-
ets — and the madness of three front doors, one glazed
in panes of primary blue, red, green that flash on the wall
at sunset splotches of elusive beauty. There is, of course,
the magnificent afterthought of five-pointed American
stars nailed up in a row under the eaves and the invention
of a round attic window, like a meaningless porthole,
which is repeated in the upper story of the barn and again
at the top of a sweet but curious outbuilding that I have
never understood. The ingenuity of domestic architecture
that accepts the endearing riddle along with the clogged
downspout, the rotten cellar door. There is a neighbor

house across a rocky field where two old sisters live, a converted oil lamp in their window, dark shades, drawn curtains, a life I cannot understand.

I am going to a high-set white clapboard house where the light shines out of a kitchen window. Always, after dark, the light reaches out across the porch and path and it strikes you with such longing though you have never lived within. I have not gone home in daylight, not once after the long visit, and I have traveled always by the back route where, if my tire blows, I will be stranded.

Going, halfway, there is a gas station. It's not that I've lied. There is the station, Good Gulf. John kicks the tires and gives me air on occasion.

"Whadda ya want to kill yourself?"

"No," but I like the slow leak, the gas tank nearly empty so that I'm driving on reserve. Why then do I stop at the gas station at all — the safety it implies with the nice man named John and his nice brother Fred. The care they take of the rest rooms. Why, going in my reckless way, do I need their good humor, good manners, good Gulf. A betrayal of everything I have come to believe is part of this grandiose adventure, going home. But no, John and Fred know me to be mild much as the world knows me; so I touch down safely at the station to gas up . . . "You're running late," they say. "Going to rain." At the station it is safe and breaks what I know to be the hysterical release of my ride home.

But wait, John and Fred do know me as the world does not — on Christmas, after useless presents, potatoes and turkey ignored, after the visit, I was going home and there they were — open at Good Gulf. Tree in the window and the colorful glare of carolers on a small television screen. "Come," they said, both Fred and John. "Have a drink." And we sat in the warm office drinking Seven and Seven from wax paper cups. And it was a happy Christmas, John having survived his operation and Fred his seizure. Mary, Fred's wife, up and about with a cane, a blessing, though John's wife, Sue, out of work. My daughter Elizabeth grown large, somber and strange. It was a bright clear Christmas Day and we talked with the volume off. John and Fred in their green work suits, and I had a red dress for the holiday visit.

It was a blessing, I said, it went on at all — my coming and going, that the two old women survived madness and boredom another year, that we all did — and filling our cups, we drank to the ladies. Fortunate, all that lay ahead: John would insulate his attic, Fred put a toilet downstairs, and I must blacktop my drive due to the rakish angle of the granite rise. We drank to the future and I toddled to the car, but not before John gave my hand a squeeze and Fred embraced me, saying what a great blessing it was not the grown kids, only his baby sick with excitement and new toys.

A good Christmas, clear, no longer bright, and thrilling to know that neither John nor Fred had given me gas or air. As I drove the back roads, the sharp winter stars appeared and I dipped well into the reserve tank, tempting fate now in a soft slippery snow, skidding at every turn, wheels spinning, drunk with delight; such a happy Christmas I counted it a blessing that I got back that night at all.

Not having died of madness. Not having died of boredom, because I take the back roads going home and believe me it is real: the still waters, the gas pump, the stop sign where only the cows may be crossing. After my visit to the ladies it is all wild distraction, I know — the hitchhikers, blowout or last sputter of fuel, the dreams, then the rescue or redemption.

I have not lied: this is real: the Regina Caeli Gift Shop where I stop going home. In a long kitchen ell of an ugly house by the side of the road. Always open and though the bells jangle as I enter, no one comes and I am left alone for a while with the candles, statues, baskets, teapots, votive lights, a smattering of antiques and many prayer books. They are selling, among other things, trust — and I remember that when I first stopped in the dead of winter I wanted to steal a bookmark or penny in a bottle, something small to prove them wrong. They had no business trusting me, and I could see them beyond the rabbit-warren rooms of the shop in the cheer of their kitchen, man and wife. I wanted suddenly a vase — a good imitation of that bloody Ming, Tang or Sung. What kind of a sanctimonious business was this that they did not come at once to sell me the brown clot-colored vase that I needed? . . . for a moderate price . . . in a tasteful shop. This was not your emporium of candles stinking of chemical gardenia and lemon tree, nor your tick-tack wickery stuff. No nibbling ceramic mice upon cheeseplates here, nor arty pots, nor the cheap paraffin, in cheaper glass, to burn for your thanks or your intentions. In the religious line no vulgarity — rather, the coarse beauty of Mexican santos, crosses honed of ivory. A Byzantine Madonna with eyes like watermelon seeds held a wizened infant in her palm. Offbeat saints, Malachy and Jude, in Alinari reproduction. Not one Vatican ashtray as a tribute to faith. This was, Queen of Heaven, all beeswax and bayberry, castile soap, white porcelain, your slab of Connemara marble for the brie. This was old sewing baskets of sweet grass, and strong new baskets of hand-split oak — the work of Victorian maidens and our American Indians of the Southwest, breeds gentle, dying, dead.

"Is anyone here?" I called to the couple sitting in the kitchen, and a man rose and came to me, a lean man with silver hair and a young rosy complexion, while behind I saw the bright steel flash of a wheelchair, a distant chalk-white face.

"This vase," I said. "It's a good color."

He said: "A good fake at least." His first words struck that note of moral superiority.

Going back, I now stop at his shop by the side of the road every trip. My needs are not material. Closing time. The end of day. Regina Caeli stays open for me with its prim convictions, my tall lean shop owner with his masked virility and the infuriating good value of his wares. Forget the beefy state trooper, forget callow Bob, squat Tom. Forget John and Fred, those boobies, and the faceless truck driver named Sam. This is a story of corruption and murder. The romantic tale of a passionate traveler.

Oh, my silver-haired lover, come lie with me. My tire has blown in front of your shop. There is no gas for miles. Drive me, then, in your simple car, to the table where

we play with a few bread crumbs in the flickering light,
to the last row of a movie we will not watch, to a park
bench in Danbury where we will take our place with the
dispossessed and drunks. Lead me to the narrow mattress
with rust stains that bleed through chilly sheets. Drive
me, though you are duty bound, in your stripped Chev-
rolet. Leave your saccharine cripple with her dry lips and
hair, her spindle limbs and useless virtue. Oh, my love,
it is spring now. The earth will yield to us. Off your shelf
I give you our text: Matthew 19 —

> For there are eunuchs born from their mother's wombs,
> there are eunuchs made by men, and those who have made
> themselves eunuchs for the kingdom of heaven. Oh, my
> dear, he that can take, let him take it.

Going home by the back route — longer. Going, it is
ill paved, narrow and steep. I have made my visit. Going,
it is longer till I see the high-set house, clapboard, white,
blood shutters, unearned nostalgia, stars, the barn porthole and peculiar outbuilding, sad neighbor house with a
life I cannot know or understand. I stop then. The light
reaches across the back porch with incredible warmth. I
have not lied, but by the time I go up the path, up the
stoop, put my hand on the knob, well, you know, I've
been somewhere.

Soup on the stove. Made out of a chicken carcass and
veal knuckles the day before. Bland then, it will not be
improved with age.

"Thank you," Maude says to her daughter, "for putting supper on." It was an effort after the exaggerations of her drive to come into the house and be genuine. Genuinely nice. Genuinely exhausted. The girl is fourteen, blunt and matronly. "Was Grandma crazy?" she asks. Quite the lady since her father died, she has set the table. She does not go to visit her grandmother. Not on Sundays. Not on holidays. The old woman has taken a dislike to her, confuses her granddaughter with a cleaning girl she once fired, orders the child to dust under beds, scolds her for the tarnished silver. So Elizabeth — she is named after her demented grandmother — Elizabeth Veronica stays alone. In the empty house she tidies, vacuums, reads: methodical and mournful. "Crazy?" she asks again. "How was your trip?"

The proper widow, Maude Dowd, looks at her peculiar child. "The trip was terrible," she cries and sits down to the dead reality of home.

From an upstairs window, her bedroom window, Maude looks out across a rocky field at the neighbor house. It is a squat old thing, flat-roofed like a coop and has been plastered over with brown and green asbestos shingles. Often Maude has been told that the house was fine, the Burr place — at one time there were gables, a decent peak to the roof, double chimneys — all the desirable attributes of a swanky Connecticut farmhouse. It is the home of two old sisters, Mattie and Jane Le Doux, and it is a blight with rotting screen porches, splintered trellises, shutters (with shamrocks and half-moons) all akimbo. In the side yard, facing Maude's house, a bathtub stands next to a quarter of a Quonset hut that arches over the Le Doux Cadillac, a gleaming white Coupe de Ville. Night and day, the low hovel of the Le Doux sisters is a mystery to Maude and she cannot dismiss it as others in town do — an eyesore, Hogan's alley. Not much as landscape, it is her view and she is drawn to it — more than to the spectacular pile of rock on the river bank across the way, Indian Rock, where (it's all too obvious) the Indians stood to watch the bend in the river; but there is no story to Indian Rock — not a lovers' tryst or massacre on the books.

Maude studies Chez Le Doux, as she now calls it — the cracked cement steps, the big barometer that she has noted (shamelessly through field glasses) is busted at ten below. The good federal house out her kitchen window does not interest her — a restoration in exquisite taste, dull pewter gray with an eighteenth-century herb garden, owned by nice men, a fabric designer and dermatologist who come to the country on weekends. Their vague, dutiful marriage centers on possessions and elaborate cooking. Nice men — they have invited Maude as a recent widow and her daughter to a dainty supper of cold apricot soup, pumpkin bread, chicken cooked with twenty-seven cloves of garlic, bitter braised endive au gratin. She feels there is no story for her in these carefully aging gentlemen, beyond the expected — their spats, minor infidelities and prolonged devotion. And though she is drawn to surfaces — their hybrid daffodils against the hand-hewn fence, their gray-green clumps of sage and yarrow — even the good taste of her own backyard does not attract Maude like the disorder of Chez Le Doux. And this morning, a brilliant day in March, the spring river riding high, grass now, buds now, this morning's promise will be fulfilled before nine o'clock.

With her back to the bedroom, Maude sees the mad filth and shambles of Le Doux as a mystery for her eyes alone. Today the first flies of the season have found the scummed saucers of milk and chipped bowls of cat food on the back stoop. Three saucers, five bowls — Woolworth junk to Costa del Sol faience to nineteenth-century pressed glass in the plain thumbprint pattern. The garbage can has been knocked over, the contents spread wide on a muddy path. Without a twinge of conscience Maude takes up her field glasses and sees the orange peels, tea bags, bank deposit slips, chicken bones, an impressive array of shimmering trays from frozen dinners. There is the pinkish cast of an antacid bottle, empty half-gallons of vodka and scotch, a cheap vermouth.

All is revealed, seemingly: trash blown across the path and into the hedges, the paltry lives of two New England spinsters in the festering homestead, pure products of America — almost. For Maude sees the fluttering envelopes in the breeze, so many, the thin blue airmail sheets, the book bags and the journals. She has seen them often on the front seat of the Cadillac by the store after Mattie has picked up the mail. Letters from all over, from the great world, addressed to Jane Le Doux. The story is this: the elder Le Doux girl is a poet, a minor poet. "Our Emily Dickinson" is the phrase used in town. A few boys and girls who go off to college come home with the news that they read old Jane Le Doux in English — usually the poignant "Rock, yield to my touch the worthless gem,"

with its fine granite-garnet imagery, a hard New England
discourse; or the short bitter lyric "Jewel Flower," with
its intense sexual anger — "Poisoned nectar, never was it
balm." Our own Emily Dickinson, the kids are told, but
no one knows what to do with Miss Jane's "pinko
poems," tough and Audenesque, about a society she has
never known, holed up as she is in Chez Le Doux. Our
own Emily Dickinson, indeed, but the town is not taken
with Jane Le Doux, b. 1900, B.A. Wellesley, lives and
writes in Shrewsbury, Conn. A few honors follow and a
long list of publications. No, the town does not really
care about their poetess, a crazy Le Doux. Well, not Le
Doux. He was some Canuck came down and married a
Burr. She's a Burr and and the Burrs were Hales and
Meekers. That's the Burr house, what's left of it. They
were all Meekers. Le Doux just came down from Nau-
gatuck and married a Burr. Jane went queer and sits in
that house writing verse, excepting rummage sales and
on rare occasions bingo. Say what you will of her madness, she's better than the fat one, Mattie.

There are no stories of thwarted love about this dry
little poetess; no married clergyman or shy farmer unable
to come to terms with the sensitivity of Miss Jane Le
Doux; and besides, the town is newly enchanted by a
novelist — a homely woman of great wealth, coarse in
all her dealings, who fantasizes stiff cocks of remarkable
dimensions performing wonders in Bel Air and high
within Olympic Towers. The town remains fascinated,
rather cruelly, by a weak handsome actor — cowboy-
cop–double agent — who cannot change a fuse or drive a

nail. There are photographers, airline pilots, drunken painters in these hills, and recently a voluptuous young woman, living by herself in a barn, whose pursed lips appear in television ads, wet and glossy.

Maude alone follows the career of Jane Le Doux. She has in her possession a sympathy note written by Miss Le Doux upon the death of her husband, Frank — lilies photographed against a purple cross: "A good man gone to God," wrote the poetess. "He was so pleasant the day he shoveled out our drive." And Maude has kept that childish note, showing it often as a charmless curiosity, though she has thrown away all other condolences as she threw away Frank's underwear, his suits and shoes, brushes and every handkerchief so that the room behind her where she sleeps on one side of a double bed is hers alone, perfectly neat with one empty closet. It is bright green and yellow, all newly decorated. The story is finished.

But what a morning! The tattered screen door of Chez Le Doux flies open and Jane, skittering like a rodent, runs down the steps and begins to gather bits and pieces of garbage — a grapefruit rind, soggy letters. What an event. The poetess is scooping up coffee grounds with a cabbage leaf. Her hair like dry ashes is pasted to a narrow skull and the garments she wears are ashen, too, a loose gray sweater and flannel skirt, the costume for the rabble in a biblical play. Darting here and there after a bottle, a bone, Jane Le Doux is seen in daylight. Maude follows with the field glasses: the small neurasthenic face of a weak child untouched by life.

Then, the back door is flung wide and Mattie greets

the day, fat and brassy, with a dome of copper hair. Jane quivers, drops a beer can and scuttles past the big body of her sister, back into the house.

Mattie seems to be laughing, as usual, that loud throaty laugh. Maude can almost hear it across the field, through the closed window of her bedroom . . . and laughing, Mattie Le Doux stretches her arms wide to a grand day. She is wearing a leopard-skin caftan with green fringe, high gold slippers, large earrings, eye shadow — at nine o'clock in the morning. It is the getup for a Puccini aria — I live for art, I live for love — or for the town whore. All Mattie's costumes are on this order, dramatic and notably garish, lime and lavender pantsuits, bright flowered shifts drawn over her big backside, iridescent boots and bangles. The town has not concerned itself with Mattie for years. One of her adventures is like another: this year's rutting in the bushes with a young carpenter, Bucky Flood, at the Democratic Picnic is of a piece with the life — a rowdy, repetitive, Boccaccian tale — the life of an idle woman once overblown and beautiful, now grotesque, who has sold off prime lots of Meeker land (not Le Doux property), land that was Burr to begin with, for her Cadillacs and trips to Vegas, Delray Beach, Acapulco. Look at the decals on the car — Virginia Beach, Fort Lauderdale, Great Adventure. Look at the latest bumper sticker: HONK IF YOU HAD ANY LAST NIGHT.

Maude is intrigued by the old girls since Frank's death. It is a harmless hobby, she tells herself, just wondering about the hours they keep and their cracked windowpanes; not true — during the past winter it's been more like an obsession. She knows each of Mattie's chunky rings, how the lipstick cakes at the corner of her mouth, the rhinestone brooch worn up to the market. She has gone to the library in New Milford and read the poems of Jane Le Doux, puzzling them out, but really at a loss. Quite independent of town opinion, in her own mind, Maude has decided that Jane is not so crazy and that Mattie is a fraud. There is something about the big woman, the extravagant dress and behavior, that is programmed, writ too large. She is a burlesque queen, not meant to be seen in the light of day.

Quickly, Maude turns and runs through the neat pretty room, her bedroom, down the stairs of the empty house, out across the rocky field, thinking simply that she will help Mattie Le Doux pick up the mess, not knowing that she is willful and meddlesome, believing that she will find in an eggshell or sodden crust direct evidence that there is — beyond the set comic roles played by Mattie and Jane — that there is a plot in Chez Le Doux, obscure, perhaps tragic, certainly compelling.

Mattie stands there in her leopard skin swinging a lamb bone. "Well," she says and notes Maude's field glasses. "You've been spying on the birds."

Maude chases onion skins, a moldy cucumber and a clump of pages. "Oh, 'Cloistered,' " Maude reads, piecing together torn pages of a handsomely printed magazine. " 'Jane Le Doux.' Why, how interesting! 'Cloistered in Connecticut.' Oh, how I would love to read it."

Then big Mattie rips the pages from her hand. "That's trash," she says. "I'd rather take them binoculars of yours and watch two robins screw."

"Oh, no," Maude says. "Please. No."

Yet another supper: Elizabeth Dowd clears the table, the few dishes and her mother's wineglass, while Maude sits on at the kitchen table playing with the napkins. She forms them into perfect tricorns, then full-blown rosettes; idle it seems, frivolous while the child works. Elizabeth knows that it is her mother wanting the meal to go on, that she should dawdle at the table and listen. ". . . just wanting to get them out in a bit of sunshine," Maude says, ". . . air and light, from the prison of those walls." It is her grandmother, the girl knows, who does not welcome air and light, but wants madly, in the stuffy dark rooms of her apartment, to die. The pots and pans are clean. The sink is clean. The drainboard scrubbed down. ". . . insensitive to her wishes or makes me feel so. The meat had gone sour and a crust of mold . . ." It is her grandmother, in stained clothes that hang off her emaciated body, who wants to starve herself — an old woman who takes her, Elizabeth Veronica, to be an incompetent serving girl named Gert — an old woman who lives on and on and on.

"I thought it might be of interest," Maude says, "on the mantel to balance the brass box and the candlesticks." There is a rustle of paper, a thump on the table. Elizabeth refuses to turn and see. What now? What next? With the greatest care she wrings the soggy dishcloth and hangs it over the faucet to dry. Another thing of interest or charm, another thing her mother has brought home. The intricate Siamese puzzle box, a scrap of faded paisley, things hand-blown, hand-turned, hand-carved. Enormous palm-leaf fans flap above the hot-air vent in the upper hall. A hideous red vase the color of scabs she'd had on her knees when she was a kid sits on the dining-room table. What next? More mirrors, another geode?

"I do not have to think of him," says Maude, "as a Christian martyr." This house is changing, full of new things. Her mother has stripped all the familiar wallpaper, painted the living room a dull green she calls celery, discarded the drapes. "It's an object of some beauty, that's all."

Elizabeth turns: there on the kitchen table is a wooden statue, a head taller than the milk carton she forgot to put away. It is a bald man, a saint in a long gown, his hand with lost fingers raised in a blessing, carved of some chalky stuff in a soft, rotting gray. She touches him. He is splintery and light as the old shingles that blow off the barn, and on one side of his face a scar of wormholes ruts down his cheek like a tear.

"He is Sicilian," Maude says, "and not very old. Nineteenth century. I'm told out of a peasant chapel, a wayside place to worship called an *ex voto*." A lecture went with each useless thing brought into the house, as though these objects, new to them, could be invested with some history to approximate intimacy and warmth. Olive wood — prized for its markings. Crackled glaze — intentional. Paisley — a manufacturing town in Scotland. "And he is no one in particular," Maude says now. "A local priest."

"Religious." Elizabeth turns the statue over in her hands. Stupid to have on the mantelpiece, as stupid as the prayers to the Dispenser of Mercy and Redeemer of Mankind said over her father's grave. "And he is a saint." She has found a piece of metal, like an old nail, that bends up from the cowl of his robe into a halo, a screwy little circle over the monk's head.

"I suppose you're right," Maude sighs. They are at an impasse, both sorry. So they have been since Frank Dowd died. Unable to speak of their abandonment, they have drawn off into private desolations. There is nothing malicious or wrong in what they say or do to each other, but there is no comfort either. The bond between them — natural, unnoticed over the years — is now like a tense, visible string in rooms, up stairs, across the table. It stretches, this love between them, strong and thin as an aerialist's wire: Maude, on her side, primps and ventures words that turn to fluff; Elizabeth stands opposite, safely armed with schoolbooks and a mop. It is a sorry business, their evenings: the hours set before them like a mild sentence. The phone seldom rings with reprieve. What now? Listen to the pump in the cellar like a heartbeat, the loose shutter whacking at an upstairs window.

"I can fix that shutter with a wire," Elizabeth says. "I can get up there on the extension ladder."

"And break an arm?" asks Maude tonight, though other nights she says a leg or that the drowsy wasps under the eaves will kill her child, but tonight it is an arm. Their precarious existence. She holds the maimed saint in her hand. Where to put him — to make him an object of interest? she asks.

"I have geometry," Elizabeth replies, "and French, social studies." To be gone from this room, this kitchen that she has cleaned like wife and mother, to leave the slight pretty woman fidgeting at the table with her toy:

Elizabeth wants to be gone with such a vengeance. I will never want anything, she tells herself, more than I want to be gone from this room now. "I have a French test, but I'll come down later and watch the news."

Elizabeth Dowd's room, her own bedroom, is plain, smudged ivory with white patches, the pale ghosts of posters. There was no further delight in the old rock stars, the baby panda, the giant redwoods reaching to the cornball sun. Elizabeth has stripped the walls. One night soon after her father's funeral she rose in a feverish sweat and stripped away the posters, the class photo, her meticulous drawings of horses and dogs, stuffed them all in the wastebasket along with lurid love notes — her big titties, jug-a-jug — from a boy on the swim team. Everything went — Pooh Bear; souvenirs of Washington, D.C., and Sturbridge Village; a little aspirin tin of marijuana seeds. It was midnight: she stood in the dim room, chilled, the clammy nightgown stuck to her belly and breasts. Satisfied that she had cleared out every scrap of childhood, she put herself back to bed. In the months that followed, her mother had brought home new bedspreads, samples of wallpaper, a digital clock. "No thanks," Elizabeth said. She was taller than her mother, with splayed womanly hips and the big bouncy tits of local fame. Her voice was steady, with a deep glottal closure as though she had finished crying or must talk firmly through a particular pain in her throat. Maude stood in the doorway of her daughter's room with her offerings — a Yale pennant, a fist of straw flowers in a cheery mug. The girl said: "I don't want them here. I have my books." True. She had taken her father's lawbooks and tax manuals and stacked them along the baseboard in neat rows.

Each night, having done up the dishes and paid some attention to her mother (in that order), Elizabeth closes the door on her plain patchy room. From a dirty canvas knapsack she draws out all her schoolbooks and stacks them beside her on the bed. The work is ridiculously simple for her at the regional school, a low building like a factory that scars the valley. She is attentive in the classes, calculating what bright answer she might give to please, withholding her disdain for the simplistic readings of American history and literature, the sluglike pace of lessons in French and math. But in her room she takes up the texts one by one, dull work.

Her father is dead, two years in his grave, buried with Yankees in the town cemetery. FRANCIS DOWD, carved into granite, the local stone. He would not have her at the regional school memorizing the mingy vocabulary lists and reproducing slovenly diagrams of Federal Govt. vs. States' Rts. and a fool seating plan of the Continental Congress. He would have her in school with *people* — the way he would say it, meaning real people — a good private school with smart kids, with green lawns and a chapel. Elizabeth fancies the cool, stony gothic of Taft School, but her father had loved the clean space, the bright rational light of Deerfield Academy. Once they had driven there on a family trip. Standing in clear New England sun, Frank Dowd had said chapel is not chapel in the old sense, never fear. It was the only time she felt bad, not being his son. She was to be sent to a girls' school, a private school up near Hartford, but Maude does not seem to remember. Her mother does not know or seem to care that Elizabeth lives with dummies all day.

On her own the girl has written to schools: she has described herself as the needy orphan of an idealistic man, a man of parts, snatched from his dear ones and a grateful body politic in the fullness of life. These self-dramatizing letters are unmailed in her dresser drawer. She cannot leave her widowed mother, who sits downstairs dealing out solitaire, not reading her serious books.

Il n'y a plus des viandes, de l'argent, de l'eau, du pain; one by one: a chapter of *Huckleberry Finn,* which Elizabeth has read some years ago, rich with details of outlawry, civic disorder, and a loathing of domesticity that would not be touched on in class; a flabby chapter of *Problems in Democracy,* imbecilic in its repeated prattle of the same misinformation. She looks, Elizabeth Dowd, to be a young matron, ample and composed as she sits up on her bed and attends to business. She is determined to attend to her schoolwork and the matters of every day — washing, eating, sleeping — with precision. She was going to a school with *people,* up near Hartford. Maybe as far away as Boston or Vermont. Now she is a poor orphan who will make her way like the brave daughter of immigrants or dirt farmers. She is the daughter of a brilliant man gone, in the fullness of life. Her correspondence with admissions officers (intimate, yet dignified) is stamped but never mailed. She has described financial woes, all imagined, a genteel background stolen from Jane Austen, a giddy, incompetent mother who is something of a borderline adult . . . *des viandes, de l'eau, du pain.* . . . She will never see the hockey fields, never honor her father by refraining from chapel prayers, never be free of her mother, that dependent, childlike woman. She will go to school with dummies and never leave the stagnant scene at the regional.

Baby Love, my Baby Love, I need you oh how I need you. The Supremes. Motown. 1966. Elizabeth rehearses for the next day. She has perfect pitch, total recall, a voice that throbs with muted pain. There is no telephone in her room, no radio. There is nothing adolescent about her as she plays her records on an old stereo, memorizing the trivial words and music with ease. There is no time to waste. No loitering after school to watch baseball practice. No sleepovers with girlfriends who laugh long into the night. There are a lot of dummies in the world. She can hear her father say that, too — with a hardness in his speech reserved for her, a warning to her that she had always taken to be love.

A lot of dummies, but Elizabeth has two years of effortless A's to show and an irreverent manner that makes her acceptable to most of the kids. *You know my love not fa-ade away,* she sings on the school bus. Buddy Holly, Brunswick, 1957. Chuck Berry. Little Richard. The Imperials. A scholar of early rock and roll, Elizabeth draws upon a seemingly encyclopedic knowledge, though her act is thoroughly researched: that amuses her. Everly Brothers. 1964. *The memory of the night before. I wonder if I'll suffer more.* She has early Elvis complete. It is impressive to the dummies, inaccessible, arcane as Latin, which is not taught at the regional. And in this way Elizabeth makes sure that she is not a freak — bookish, subdued, that's all, a little hefty in the hips since her father's death. Older in some way kids cannot define, she gives them the immediate past of a simple world they care about. "Maybellene." "Peggy Sue." "Don't Be Cruel." Did you know Johnny Maestro sang lead in the Rhythm Method? And she gets her kicks singing for them on the school bus. There is a touch of the show girl about her as she straddles the aisle and belts out "Stop! In the Name of Love," careening up Painter Hill Road.

Her mouth, though she makes sure to score highest on all vocabulary tests, is fashionably foul. "Asshole," she says of the principal, Mr. Muckler. "Fuck-ups," the librarians. "Piss-poor," the glee club. It's the way they all talk, the dummies.

Each night she stuffs the books back into her khaki bag and throws it across the room with a thud, then gets her act down, singing like a pro to the old albums. Next Elizabeth swivels the hot bullet of her reading lamp up to the ceiling. The room is palely washed, the light refracting in a soft aureole on the empty floorboards, the single bed, the grim line of lawbooks. From the back of her closet, under games and puzzles, she draws out a large box. It pictures a boy and girl in ecstasy over an optics set with test tubes and microscopes glittering behind them. In the box there is a man's shirt and tie, a plastic bag with personal effects. They were labeled personal effects in the hospital: her father's watch, ring, pocket comb, his wallet.

Now she spreads the shirt out on her bed, a yellow cotton, fine but everyday, the way he looked every day, powerful, a big gruff man seducing the world. Then the tie, dark blue silk woven with mallards in flight — she tucks it under the collar, draws the knot tight. Elizabeth bends to the man, her head upon his wide breast, holding his two dimensions as they sway close. Once they danced like that at a wedding when she was a little girl. It is the dance that will never end. No tears, sobs, words, never — a blankness of loss, control as she reaches for the clear plastic bag and sets out the ring that was found rattling around with Frank Dowd's change in his coat pocket. To the greater glory of God (she has translated that): Loyola High, 1948; crudely faceted stone, cheap token of good luck. Bulova watch, which she winds, spreading flat the brown leather band stained with his sweat . . . comb with gray grease from his hair like satin to her touch . . . wallet, frayed at the edges, entirely satisfactory its bulk and shine. Elizabeth strokes the credit cards long canceled, the driver's license — Francis J., eyes brown, 6′2″, organ donor, but there is no one alive with her father's kidneys or eyes. Here there is twenty-seven dollars, his last bank-deposit slip and a note she reads nightly, unfolding the creased blue paper, which has almost fallen into little squares:

Frank,
If you can't get the Debussy "Images" in New Haven, forget it.
Love you anyway,

> *Claire*

The difficult part now: to fold the note away and think nothing. Elizabeth thinks of nothing at all, though some nights it goes through her head, rising through experienced blankness, that her father knew nothing of Debussy, nothing at all. Next untie the tie, fold the shirt. Large Elizabeth, ample as a brood hen, packs up her kit and stows it under the puzzles and games. There is no clock in her room, but her father's watch, the band stained with his sweat in the darkness, reads nearly ten o'clock. It is time to take her shower, then attend to her mother: watch the news.

Downstairs, Maude has put her blessed statue on the mantel with brass candlesticks — churchy. Without the candlesticks — insignificant. She has read to the end of her murder mystery and already forgotten the plot. She has draped a paisley shawl over a table, tried the saint there under an imposing terra-cotta lamp. That effect is woolly and hot. The window is open in the living room where Maude fusses, the first possible night for a breath of air, and the light earthy smell pleases her. The rush of the swollen river, just within hearing, is soft at this distance. She is ready for something, perhaps only the change of season. Passing the time she has set out a "serious" book along with her mystery story as she does each night, and the bills to be paid, a widow's fancy of purpose. Then Maude settles in a corner of the couch, draws into herself. She is little with a fine small body, like a miniature dog bred for show. She turns her fluffy bright head about the room checking the pretty setup she has seen a thousand times. Her idleness seems defiant as she lets the time pass, turning pages but not willing to read or to write checks. Nestled in her parlor, Maude dwells on the man who sells her whatever at the Queen of Heaven Gift Shop, his silver hair, his body that is trim, a widow's fancy. He comes toward her and her own body quivers like a dreaming animal's . . . from the hips, as though he is dancing to her, coming around all the fragile glass and metal cabinets, then pressing her . . . there is nowhere in the jumble of artifacts, not down in the dust of a doormat. There is nowhere possible . . . her bucket seats or muddy patch on the highway. His hair is still dark where it curls over the collar of a peasant shirt he wears, like a girl's. A field . . . he will take her money . . . a green field: in a naive scheme Maude forces a field already soft with new grass and the calendar joys of buttercups and distant horses. He will take her money . . . the wife asleep in the back room or at some humdrum devotions. Water, the long placid lake, Lillinonah. Beyond the docks and fuel pumps a rock in the sun, water below. Her bare body on warm rock, smooth granite washed in the sun, tender as mown grass: large like a bed tilted up from the water's edge their rock lies. Her bare body and his. They lie ageless, of course not young. He has taken money from her, coming at her around counters, pressing her accidentally like some man on a bus when she was working, a girl. She had her change and the sight of his crotch to take home, a gift she's paid for.

"I never hoped," he says. The gentle wilt of his penis blooms in the bright light.

"Well, I did. And I thought — here on the rock at Lillinonah, naked in the sun to feel you. I thought for weeks coming into the shop, watching you close the door to your kitchen, closing her out, poor thing, when I came. You do that now, close the door on that life and we are alone. You knew there would be commerce between us. Why can't you take my money without looking at the floor, coughing, fluttering my bills?"

His cock is stiff. Up at a proud angle and his balls, she can see, are tight, ready for her. She stretches away from him seductively, the warm rock caresses her in surprising places. "You are in business," she says as he mounts her in the sun. "Take my money."

"I worked in the city for twenty years."

Getting personal, she'd asked him. To her it is as if he'd said, "Now, I must have you," or "Your eyes are sad and beautiful." She remembers his words as a passionate disclosure: "I worked in the city for twenty years. Then we came up here."

Reckless, she'd said: "My husband is dead." How had she worked that in? Matter-of-fact, holding a gentleman's gift item in her hand, a Florentine box for cufflinks Frank never used. And she'd said further that she loved Italy, to show what? Her sophistication, to the man she meant to pursue until he had her pinned naked on a rock. In the sun.

A breeze comes in at the window flapping the curtains and Maude looks up, startled to see the lights still on at Chez Le Doux. Jane, it must be, writing by the converted oil lamp. It's not the porch light left on for Mattie out drinking at the Log Cabin. Not tonight. The back end of the Cadillac gleams like a white Charlevoix cow in the moonlight. Where do they sit all the hours at night in their squalid house? This does interest Maude but she is too lazy to run upstairs and grab the binoculars. She

would like to confirm that it is the shadow of the fat
sister pouring another drink, to trace the silhouette of the
skinny sister bent over an old desk. Do they speak? Mattie, laughing, must tell of her latest glorious rut in the
motel on Rte. 7, while Jane spouts fresh lines of verse. It
is spring — time for love, poetry, madness, but ordinar-
ily it is dark at Chez Le Doux well before ten o'clock.

The saint is now on the coffee table blessing a new
crystal ashtray, magazines, household bills and the serious book. She has chosen the book because of her man,
picking it off a shelf in the Queen of Heaven, turning its
pages flirtatiously in front of him: a popular history of
the fourteenth century. She has reason to believe there
will be God in the book, Mary, disease, redemption, but
she doesn't give a damn for that. She hates his piety. The
bald spot in his silver hair reminds her of a tonsure. Wed
to grief, pain, abstinence — he has begun to wear sandals
on warm days. Meek they look and humble like a men-
dicant's footwear. The handwoven smocks he affects,
open at the neck to display the sacred medal of a discredited saint. That she will take off him, too. Naked.
She means to have him stripped. It is only a matter of
time till they cross the green field to her rock. The phone
rings in the silent house.

"She's in bed now and did, indeed, hide the pill under
her tongue again, but I caught her at it." Maude, thinking
still that she will take the medal off her lover with some
violence, listens to her mother's nurse. "She's going on
about Sonny. Who's he? 'Sonny's down cellar,' she says."

"Her cousin, Sonny Walsh." Maude remembers him,
almost illiterate, a shuffling, wisecracking old cousin,

flabby, diabetic, eating sugar doughnuts at the kitchen table. Wonderful man. "Sonny fixed the furnace and the boiler, a wonderful man."

"She's asleep, unless she's playing games. We never know, now do we?"

"No, we never know," Maude agrees with that. Tonight Belle Petry sounds sober, her speech clear and snappy, but she holds her liquor well in any case, Southern Comfort that she keeps behind the soup cans. Maude would drink, too, confined with her mother, wandering the few rooms of that stale apartment. "Get some rest, Belle."

Belle says, "I'm all right, kiddo. I've got to do my nails and with the weather warm now I got to do my toes." Belle is eighty-three with swell legs and small feet. Crouched on the bed in her tiny half-room with folding doors, she will paint her fingers and toes a new shade of rust-rose. From a suitcase under the bed she will get out her summer sundresses and high-heeled sandals. Belle has no place to go.

Maude has the lights to put out in the kitchen, the locks to turn, both front and back. Upstairs she hears Elizabeth's music now, the thump of it — the wail of that awful music, she says to her friends, to Belle Petry, to anyone in the Post Office or store who will listen, pretending maternal annoyance: she is actually delighted when her daughter livens up the house with any normal teenage nuisance. Though it is always so precise. She could set a clock by the first blast of Elizabeth's music. Soon it will be time for the news. Only a matter of time until she gets her man, hunts him down in the half-light of his shop, in the smell of sandalwood and orange meant to cover must. A tomb for his angels and Mary — heaven brought down to this dank shop, his own saint wheeling from sink to pantry. She will corner him, have him out in the air, full sun, naked, pale, his member rising in the palm of her hand.

Oh, she knows his game, her shopkeeper. You display the best goods when you no longer believe. Frank had tried that with the shredded ends of his Catholicism — lived on a rich diet of Latin, the church fathers, Graham Greene. He had brushed up his Dante and Cardinal Newman when he should have mastered contracts and evidence. In their first apartment in New Haven. Then he was able to say to her, I believe in the history, the continuity, while she, sacrilegiously, threw away a broken chain of rosary beads from the bottom of her purse as an obsolete charm. She would not be his little wife telling her beads. She would not go with him to see the manuscripts in the rare-book room of the University, pulling aside the faded curtain to gaze upon the vellum and gold, the scrolling handwrought letters encompassing demons and virgins. She could take them as a tribute to man's artistic accomplishment, Frank said, if she did not like real prayers. On their first Christmas he bought her a coffee-table book of fleshy Madonnas as something of a truce, all lusty ladies among fruits and vegetables. See, he said, the history, the continuity, and she saw these women of the High Renaissance in velvets and brocades, holding healthy babies, smug in their secular world. It was before they had Elizabeth, in New Haven, when Frank silently gave up the show of mass at Saint Brendan's — that was the name of the parish — as though that hour a week could not be stolen from his work. Ritual arguments between them were substituted for the rituals of faith: so much energetic talk about birth control, divorce, abortion — foreign it seemed to her now, her girlish rebellion. It was years before they had Elizabeth. Their moral dilemmas had drifted out of her mind like French, her best subject in school, material she did not use in her adult life: the careful discriminations faded away like the sexual life of her early marriage until there was nothing left but a record of experience — a curriculum vitae, not the feeling or vocabulary itself.

She knows his game, the man she wants with the bald spot, but she does not know his name. He looks to Maude like a lean Jew or Spaniard, his thin nose humped in the middle, his high rosy complexion, his eyes nearly black and the eyelids stained dark. Untroubled, a look of unearthly calm on his face, of a sweetness that was not manly, quite. Sandals and smocks. He has come up from the city. Now he hurries from the back of the shop to meet her, closing the door behind. Nurse to his wife. It is only a matter of time. He expects her Tuesday and Thursday — early evening — Sunday afternoon. After the visit. Maude has a daughter: she tells him this, getting personal, and a mother afflicted with a wandering mind. He has come up from a brownstone in the Village, hopeless the stairs for his hopeless wife. There is such a torrential . . . well, flush of pleasure between them. That's not her fancy. He, of course, knows her name because it is written on her checks.

Just as she settles to the couch again and picks up the

serious book, Elizabeth appears with wet hair and a bath-
robe gathered around her body looking like a big farm
girl, one of those pathetic kids married out of high school,
finished at twenty. But that's wrong. Elizabeth has been
locked in her room studying. She is purposeful and dull,
Maude feels, her youth gone. Helpless with her daughter
in the room, she sits until the girl says sharply, "Time
for the news." They watch from a television set hidden
in a commode, here in the living room Maude has made
into a mock Victorian parlor no family could live in.

"What will you wear tomorrow?" Maude asks her
daughter.

Elizabeth shrugs. She hates her mother's attempts to
make her a cute kid, a girl in those advertisements with
little outfits. Clothes must cover her body, that's all. She
despises the slick magazines her mother reads, turns the
pages in disgust at the gamboling girls, some of them in
fresh green fields, so unlikely . . . others real, suppos-
edly real, with briefcases, careers and dilettantish interests
in photography and politics. Elizabeth hates the
dummies.

There has been a fire in the Bronx. Babies are passed
out of windows. An old black woman describes the blaze
with lilting passivity as relatives and neighbors crowd behind her on the screen: "The children, my daughter Van-
da's, aged three and four, I hear crying in the back room
with the baby. The paint is blistering off the kitchen
walls." The charred tenement appears as a gate of hell.
Entrance to a summer of arson, violence, racial strife: the
prediction of a brisk young woman tapping a pencil
against papers, the props of a journalist on display. Eliz-

abeth hates her, ambitious parrot in her beautiful dress and beads . . . a dummy. She looks at her mother, at the closed book: another evening wasted. The hours drain from her mother's life in a sloth that had gone on for years . . . years before her father's death.

There is a report on Ping-Pong diplomacy. Chairman Mao and his wife are nodding, smiling at a mixed bag of Americans, our champs. It is all lightweight, the new friendship, hollow as a bouncing table-tennis ball. China looks gray on the color television screen. The Americans with flight bags and cameras wear red jackets: eager, as yet undefeated. Now Elizabeth misses her father and tries with a moan to assume his wry attitude, the contempt he would have had for "noodle rapprochement." After his death there had been her mother's fury, tearing the house apart until every stain and chip of the past was gone. Then she had lapsed again into idleness, though there continue the visits to oversee the old age and madness of Grandma Fain. Once heartbreaking to the child, she sees that her mother's duty is now routine.

"You should get a haircut," Maude says. Elizabeth knows that her mother is smooth and powdered, shaved clean on the legs, slick under the arms. The down over her lip is bleached; brows tweezed to neat unreflective arches. She wears a deep herbaceous scent to sit here alone. There is her mother sitting like a pet with her feet tucked up under her. Elizabeth can no longer say if her mother is pretty. She cannot read much of anything in the limited range of expressions that appear on Maude's face, though sometimes there is a movement of the eyes, bright and interested, as though she watches changing scenes. Tonight she seems entirely vacant — dressed in a little outfit, peachy gold to go with the false amber glow of her hair: rings, bracelets, chains in place. Elizabeth feels responsible for this woman who sits alone on the couch in a ghastly perfection.

She says: "I *should* get a haircut." They smile at each other across the room.

Maude has forgotten the news, the weather report. "What was the weather?" she asks.

"Some clouds."

"It doesn't matter," Maude says. "Tomorrow I don't have to go."

Then the girl kisses her mother goodnight, her long damp hair slapping at Maude's cheek. She smells the powder, the paint, the oppressive perfume her mother wears, suffocating as dark rooms in daylight.

Mrs. Fain gets out of bed. It is night — anytime from sunset to dawn. The big hooded lights in the parking lot shine into her window. She is on the third floor in a one-bedroom apartment but does not know it. The rug is hers, an old Kerman bought by her father when their house was built. Mrs. Fain is not in her house but in this strange place, painful, with clumsy venetian blinds and no proper moldings around the doors and windows. Against the sallow walls the blinds throw streaks of light that make her eyes go. It is maddening to her and she marches to the window and clatters them up by their dirty cords. Cheap things the new people down the block bought after the war, metallic and cold, hard to clean. She has always preferred dark green shades of heavy linen on her windows and there is a man left on the East Side who makes them still, a German named Kieller who makes them still with heavy rollers.

Below is a narrow parking lot no bigger than her double drive all filled with cars. Her own green Chrysler is kept up. One of the first cars without a shift, she keeps it up and it sits below. (It does not, for she drove it off without enough gas, or off at odd hours and forgot to come back here, here to this place.) There is a chain fence below — certainly not her choice. A decorative iron fence is more to her liking, if one must when the neighborhood changes, then an iron fence with gentle twines and curves. Below a small park — queer, no bigger than her own backyard. Mrs. Fain enjoys the trees leafing out, though in the breeze with the glare lights they make her eyes go. An unused park, no more than two corner lots with benches. A man in slippers pulls a large white dog along the path to the stone post, a marker for the King's Highway that has been there all her life. 24 M. NEW HAVEN, it says. Mrs. Fain scorns old news: she knows she is twenty-four miles from New Haven.

Now she dresses, taking off a peculiar blue nightgown that is not hers, no more than the waxy yellow shoulders are hers or these scrawny legs mapped out with veins. She has thick legs, no problem now but tragic when she was a girl. She finds her own undershirt and lisle pants, her wool skirt, sweaters, heavy stockings and bulbous orthopedic shoes. Mrs. Fain is ready to cook a leg of lamb. She will not trust the lamb to Gert, a simpleton whom she must fire. Gert has cracked the punch bowl. Gert has polished silver with steel wool. Mrs. Fain must cook the

lamb herself, but first the big mirror over her dresser tells
her that her hair . . . and she knows how untidy, how
thin and pokes at her head with pins and combs. She has
a wad of hair like matted wool in the hair receiver and in
the bottom drawer behind a girdle and some greeting
cards she has saved a bag of her own hair. She will have
a rat made or hairpiece to puff it up. Once there were
two bags but Maude threw one out or Gert, Gert threw
it out. Now another tuft of yellowed white strands to
pull off the comb, to wad into the receiver with her ini-
tials *VEF* on ivory celluloid etched in black, the elongated
modernistic letters that make her eyes go. That was a
present from the man she married.

In the hallway it is dark but something tells her no
lights. She carries her purse and wool gloves that are cozy,
stealing past pictures of babies and wedding parties that
erase themselves in the dark and on into the miserable
kitchen with tinny cabinets and an oven, which is not
hers, stuck in the wall. Still, there is nothing nicer than a
leg of lamb. Mrs. Fain turns the oven to 350 and gets out
the roasting pan she has had since 1928. She makes herself
toast with marmalade. She eats: it is an old habit. Dreaming into the days of May and June that face her on Tom
Grillo's insurance calendar, she nibbles the crust only.
Food does not taste much in this place.

"God help us!"

There is that woman — some prize lady, Mrs. Fain calls
her — shoving past her to the oven.

"You'll kill us both," Belle Petry says and Mrs. Fain is
led out of the galley kitchen full of fumes into the dim
parlor. "A social hour," Belle says. "It's three-thirty in

the morning. Finish your toast." Belle is not cross. They could surely have died, but what matter. It is only a matter of days or weeks, a matter of time. The nurse draws her pink kimono to her as she opens the windows wide — no need, for it is a spring night soft as Miami, but with the smell of churned New England earth from flower beds in the park below and soon she will not be here to miss the warmth at night. "Dr. Petry loved these warm nights in Miami," she says, and there is a little catch near her heart like a tick.

Mrs. Fain does not believe the prize lady in pink knows beans about Florida. She's been there often enough with her father or perhaps her husband and has a white shawl from Montaldo's, Palm Beach, to prove it.

"Dr. Petry loved his siesta and then stayed up late on the warm nights, Spanish hours."

"Is this your toast?" Mrs. Fain asks. It is this woman's toast, the prize lady always coming here wanting marmalade on her toast. Mrs. Fain does not like sweet things herself. Sweet nothings, Sonny said, for there was diabetes in her family. She must tell her children — Maude and Kevin. Kevin was the one. It must always be that way — one child so satisfactory with his baseball and rough manners, the other tiresome and bossy. It was Maude drove off her Chrysler. Maude brought that Gert into the house and this fine lady. She would not tell Maude there was diabetes in the family. One aunt, a nephew, and Sonny, who drank Coca-Cola and kept candy bars in the drooping pockets of his pants. "This must be your toast," says Veronica Fain politely to the old woman who sits across from her smoking a cigarette, her beautiful legs crossed, high satin slippers dangling from her painted toes.

"Eleven, twelve o'clock at night he'd say let's walk out under the palms, Belle. Dr. Petry loved an ocean breeze and it was perfectly safe then. Of course, it was safe always with Dr. Petry well over six feet and fine build to the end. He just looked at any man or woman in his way," says Belle, who eats a bite of toast now to please Mrs. Fain. Tonight if she had slept through that gas they'd both be gone, simply gone and she would talk no more of the old man she married, a retired surgeon, whose modest savings she has outlived. Belle with her R.N. and fortunate looks, her lives upon lives and the achievement of ten dignified years with Dr. Petry. If she had slept, poor Mrs. Fain, shivering in her woolen clothes, wandering this painful place, would be warm, untroubled, perhaps gathered to her father's house, a solid house with many rooms much like the house she kept for Dr. Petry. But they are awake in the last of the fumes and Belle leads Mrs. Fain back to the bedroom.

She will not tell Maude of their exciting scrape with death, the roast unroasted — that pathetic creature with her neutered widow's ways, her life a series of distractions, hustling down to visit them, duty plastered on her wan face. The pretty clothes for nothing, figure for nothing. Belle has a picture of Maude in mind, all dressed up poking through her mother's refrigerator and personal papers with disapproving sighs, rummaging through the old woman's clothes to set order where none can be had.

Taking the layers of wool off Mrs. Fain, who sits smiling on the bed, Belle Petry thinks of the twenty years, not bad, since the summer afternoon in 1951 when the Doctor did not wake up from his siesta. Keep the undershirt, dear, and the long lisle pants if they're a comfort. Take the crust of toast between your fingers, dear. Belle knows the secret of making them easy and she pours medicated lotion into her palm and begins to work it into the wasted thighs and thin old legs, gently rubbing, rubbing the old lady's skin so slick, yellow — and clean though she cannot get Mrs. Fain to wash and why bother? What Belle needs now is a good tipple to get her through to daylight, double dose, but she works on rubbing the old toes, the cold soles of the feet. She loves Veronica Fain, loves tending to her body — Belle Petry's last case. Her patient draws herself up like a child, smiling, and seems to sleep. There is the tick again at Belle's heart, a swift constriction, then the miraculous passing of death. She would like one last outing — dinner and a drink. She needs lip pomade, stockings. It is spring: Mrs. Fain's daughter will drive her; and she would like one last word before she dies — to tell that Maude to settle down, to pay attention to someone or something.

Determined, Maude goes upstairs carrying the serious book. Elizabeth's door is closed against her and she seeks the pale carpet of her own room, still new to her the youthful paper of green and yellow garlands looped to the ceiling. Frank would have hated it all. There is a sweetness here he would not abide, a delicacy left from her girlhood, a taste for ruffles and piecework quilts her marriage had not destroyed. No man comes in this room. Unlike the sturdy old-fashioned aspects of the house, the strong nostalgic pull of attic and barn, Maude's room is merely quaint. Naked, in the light of her newest lamp, she opens the windows wide and hears the river across the road, its angry ineffectual assault on Indian Rock, and then turns to check out Chez Le Doux. It is ablaze, all windows lit. With quiet urgency the headlamp of an ambulance sweeps the field. Men come and go up the cracked cement steps with mysterious equipment from the high white ambulance that sits silent in the drive.

Maude is terrified, as though it is her very life. Which one? Jane or Mattie — and she hears Mattie, the big laugh like a wail, a hoot of pain, sees her at the back door holding it open as the men carry out Jane on a stretcher, gray mouse covered in death completely with a gray blanket, gone with her small fame. Maude grabs for her clothes. She must go there, but as she dresses, the cars drive up to Chez Le Doux. They will be Meekers, Hales — family. They will be Burrs. Family of Jane Le Doux. It was a life she never knew or understood, but Maude is moved to tears. She will not tell Elizabeth, who is disgusted with her prying into Le Doux affairs. In the morning she will call her friends but now she cries in private feeling that she did at least try to imagine that life when no one else cared.

In bed Maude finally opens her book, a distraction, and has to laugh: the chapter is about death, the Black Death in particular, the devastation of cities in the fourteenth century. Before the first case of the infection was actually diagnosed in Strasbourg the Jews were murdered for polluting wells, the clothes torn from their backs in hopes that they were concealing gold. In Padua. In Florence.

Corpses piled in the streets, ignorance and filth, blind faith. The loose shutter whacks the house. She will never let Elizabeth climb the extension ladder to fix it. Maude can read only a few pages of her book, not because the text is brutal or the death of her neighbor is sad, but because the book is hard, full of hard facts — charts, footnotes in medieval Latin or French. She's bought history from him not thinking, or thinking only of her man in his shop with the big package, big cock, humped nose, her man under the sign of Mary, Queen of Heaven, our sweetness and hope. Her serious reading is about him, about his infuriating goodness that sets him apart and spoils her dreams. Anyway it is comforting to read that laborers took advantage of the plague, knowing they were scarce; they disdained cold cabbage with penny ale and demanded fresh flesh or fish, piping hot. Like a high-school girl learning football plays and the terminology of soccer to please a boy, she reads the history book, a few pages. Fifty thousand dead in Venice, sixty-five in Milan, her neighbor dead, a desolation unequal . . . there is no proportion. Maude, like an adolescent girl, will be ready to talk to her lover about monastic rule, trade routes, the rise of the middle class. She stretches until her bones crack, stretches out on the double bed and waits with her legs flung wide.

Under her pillow Mrs. Fain has a bag of vanilla cookies, which she eats at dawn. Something tells her to suck the sweet brown edges of her cookies in bed. The streetlamps go off and a colorless brittle light enters the room — that makes her eyes go. On the narrow windowsill is

the Bavarian stein her father bought for the plate shelf
and would not hide during the war. How they hated the
Huns. *You can capture him with ease. Offer him a little bit of
Limburger cheese.* She was too old to spank but her father
shamed her and the stein remained in the dining room on
display right up through the Armistice and beyond: cav-
aliers drinking at an inn, flanked by blond maidens, the
top of hinged pewter mounted with a jolly German friar.
It was Sonny in that war. Stupid as he was, she loved
him, her cousin — a stout boy, no brains and a sweet
tooth. How they laughed sucking sugar cubes in the barn.
He went off in a straw hat and his Sunday suit to war
. . . she must tell Maude, always coming with a sour
face . . . resplendent in his suit and white shoes her father bought him. Sonny Walsh. They were singing at the
railroad station when he left and he kissed her. Such a
moment for Veronica with braids still down her back.
Mayor King parading from the Court House. The nurses
veiled like nuns. Laughing, but there were tears in his
eyes, the big lummox, for her, not the war, for Vee —
and she pressed a bag of licorice on him. A young lady
when he came back. Away at college. And Sonny went
to work for her father doing menial tasks. From their
new positions they joked a little. *You can quickly bring him
out. Offer him a little bit of hot sauerkraut.* He could not read
much or write, could never sit still long. It was not till
she had children that he came to fix her faucet and the oil
burner in her new house — whatever else; bringing his
own Coca-Cola and the candy bars stuffed in his pockets,
the pants swaying from old suspenders — and then they

laughed. "Vee, you was a swell girl till they put a rod up your arse." Oh, Sonny, don't — don't make me laugh. "Well, what'd they teach you anyway? They march me around in the sun with a rifle in the straw hat and stiff collar and I got no uniform till I'm on the other side." No man like him, only Kevin with his rudeness and his fun. And Sonny drove an old Ford car around town putting his foot right through the floorboards like a clown, spitting cigar juice, harmless to silly young girls and every dog, a genius with drain pipes, motors, electric wire. Filthy teeth. Grizzled beard. "The doctor says it's diabetes, Vee, but low as I feel, I say it's change of life." Oh Sonny, Sonny — don't make me laugh.

Maude comes to visit her mother on the highway. The direct route coming down passes the necessary shopping centers and the housing developments growing one into another north from the city. One dilapidated church and an old vegetable stand remind Maude that years ago on Sunday drives this was the country. The rest is new, a serviceable landscape that she might find anywhere in America. No mysteries in the Lafayette Mall or the turn-off to Glenn Road East, Woodside Drive, Devon Estates. Coming, she wants no surprises. Bowling alleys, used-car lots, a couple of bad Chinese restaurants — the worst is predictable. The highway is fast, a dull drive for Maude. Coming to see the old women, she understands her duty and imagines little else. She pulls off at the North Avenue exit, turns left around the little park and into the lot,

where she looks up at her mother's windows. It is there
they pace the rooms, the venetian blinds all cockeyed.
Coming up on the elevator she is calm, but at the door,
key in hand, she is amazed to find them bickering and
still alive.

SORROW

ENTOMOLOGISTS predict that the infestation of gypsy moths will be three times that of preceding years due to the mild winter,' " Maude Lasser read aloud.

"Vagaries of the Gulf Stream," said Bert. He sat with his wife in the bedroom of their apartment overlooking the Hudson. The sky was stretched taut behind their view of New Jersey, a flawless steel blue, but the river was fierce, both dark and glittering in the winter sun, mottled with whitecaps. One ship, very white with blue funnels, made the graceful pivot out of its dock.

In a creaking basket chair with frayed pillows, Maude read the *Times,* throwing an item to Bert now and then as he turned through notes for a lecture he would give in Texas the next day. She loved the ability her husband had to break from true work and answer every question or proposition that came his way, as though he should be able to balance a broom on his nose and sing like any fool.

"It was greed," Bert said, "that brought the gypsy moth to this country. A Frenchman with a respectable academic career went for the big money." At his podium, Maude thought. She should really install a blackboard on their bedroom wall. "Silkworms don't live in this climate so Leopold Trouvelot thought he'd breed them with the *Lymantria dispar* in a backyard in Medford, Massachusetts. Feed them mulberry leaves. It was the naive enterprise of a third-rate nineteenth-century scientist with ignoble commercial dreams. When the moths escaped it was worse than anything he imagined. No silk. Certainly no glory."

Maude said: "They were terrible the year my mother died." A look of terror that was real crossed her face, and Bert, who had heard this before, knew it was no idle complaint. "They were all over the windshield, the grocery bags. I found caterpillars down in my dress and in Elizabeth's ear. Everywhere."

"They are nasty but relatively harmless." And that was Bert being reasonable. He returned to the untidy manuscript before him. It was his comfort to tell her the parable of the gypsy moth and the failed Frenchman, to soothe her with facts. But the caterpillars were truly terrible. She had never forgotten the pale brown worms of that year and their droppings — on the back of her hands, spinning down into her hair — from diseased branches everywhere. Maude watched her husband switch back to the mess of papers and scrawl illegibly between lines, down margins. In all other respects he was a neat man: trim with exercise, tan from a recent trip to the Mideast, something of a dandy. He sat across from her in the other creaking basket chair and took the first phone call of the day.

It was 9:03. Gilbert Lasser was dressed in a vested dark gray suit, a shadow plaid, his boots gleaming, his collar pinned high. So much spit and polish — Maude thought her husband looked military, an officer in mufti, though he mistrusted the military, naturally. But she placed him earlier in the century, a retired colonel keeping track of the Empire still. That is how he looked with the prim knot in his regimental tie, his clipped gray beard and hair cropped close like lamb's wool. Intense as Freud, she thought, before the great man was worn out. Which contradicted the British-colonel image, of course: one of her muddles.

"Don't romanticize me," Bert would say and tell her he was genetically blessed with a fine metabolism and that his love of clothes came from the humiliation of being dragged around by his father when he was a kid, shoved up the stairs to lofts on lower Broadway — that whole area below the Flatiron Building — for a deal. An ill-cut pair of pants, a cheap yellow-green suit, an imitation herringbone jacket with imitation leather patches on the elbows. Fake ties on elastic bands. For his bar mitzvah a white tuxedo that sported satin stripes missewn on the inside of the trousers. Who's gonna see? Keep your pants on. Always some grubby deal. A cousin's uncle got underwear half-price. Imagine the nickel-and-dime economics of it. No, Bert Lasser wanted his clothes straight, from haughty salesmen at good shops, expensive haute-bourgeois fare. As for the Empire, that was foolish: he lived now. Maude knew this to be true, that it was a matter of pride to him that he lived now, now with the earth sliding into the sea and the clock ticking against doom for the mountain laurel, condor, the great leviathan. Now with acid rain and the demise of public transportation, in an ungovernable nation that he said was four countries at least. He sat across from her talking to a travel agent, his secretary, a geneticist — all the while scribbling in the margins, insisting in so many words that we must work against that fashionable cliché — entropy. And he read a bit to Maude, what he'd say in Texas. He was for raising wheat on arid soil, distribution of grain — a shift of power by simply embracing obvious technology. It was, in recent months, his scenario for the possible. Bert in his plaid suit, accountable like an English gentleman of another time — so she was right. Bert Lasser overseeing it all.

"Oh, no — 'a thousand eggs to a single mass,' " Maude read. " 'The moths die after mating. They have no adult life.' "

"Perhaps you will get some satisfaction out of that," said Bert.

The next call was hers: Elizabeth — restless, pregnant with her first child in Westchester, was about to drive into the city on a foolish errand. Surely they had Italian sausage out there, but Elizabeth's breasts were swollen, her back strained when she sat in the empty house. Gus had gone on his commuter train. The weather was fine. She would be in the house for the rest of her life. Wasn't it better to buy sausage and cheese on Broadway while she still fit behind the wheel of the car?

"Look," Maude said as she hung up the phone. The white cruise ship was directly in view, plying its way out to sea, whiter than they expected, with flags snapping, festive streamers on deck. From their distance there was much the Lassers could not see — the cargo of pale vacationers, overdressed, spiffy, anxiously starting the fun: the pineapple and coconut drinks laced with rum being ladled out gratis on the chill enclosure of the foredeck. They could not hear the cynical fakery of the steel band with its endless shuffle of marimbas softly abrasive in the skull. Yet a smile passed between them, a fine complicity, for they had been married happily for five years and from this window safely watched the cruise ships sail by.

"I can't even imagine it," Maude said, though she had imagined it in great detail: the enforced idleness, the shipboard flirtation, sex with unsuitable partners, sunburn. The Lassers had thought what a nightmare to be trapped on one of those pleasure boats, held hostage with strangers following the sun to duty-free shops, nite-spots, contemptuous natives.

"It's dangerous in those Caribbean ports," Bert said. "One day they will be killed."

To Maude that was an acceptable idea. Her list of horrors included retirement villages, resorts with tasteful shops and a heavy population of Mercedes, most of Southern California, Hawaii and the suburban splendor of her daughter's life. What Bert never quite got was how deeply his wife feared purposeless days. It was 9:20, a late start.

Maude pulled on a respectable sweater, found a pair of shoes. She went to the door with her husband, who had the morning in his office at the Foundation, lunch with a Palestinian doctor, the Texas speech to finish before his plane. What a sport he was in his twill overcoat with velvet collar, a snap brim hat, umbrella furled.

"The sun's out," Maude said.

"Long-range prediction." And he held the umbrella up smartly like a swagger stick.

"Oh, nuts," Maude said and gave him the morning kiss, which today was a kiss good-bye.

Alone, she goes to a small back office. Once a maid's room, it still has a dinky washbasin in the corner. A window looks out on a ledge of pigeon droppings and down to a desolate courtyard below. Pebbles and weeds. Light from years ago seems entrapped in the empty space, a dim vista of New York for foreign girls and black women. With the curtains drawn and soft lights, Maude feels her patients never guess; the love seat, an easy chair, the basket of books and toys, pictures of flowers, Dürer's rabbit — nothing unpleasant, as she has arranged it. From a locked file she draws out a folder — WARREN BIDART — and as she waits for her cue her hands smooth the pages of notes she no longer needs to read. In the little office a bell rings calling her to attention. Startled, she hurries to the door of the apartment, where Warren plays dead in the hall, his baby face hidden with a scarf and wool hat.

"He can't stand your elevator," says Mrs. Bidart. The Bidarts live in an apartment house on the East Side with fountains in the lobby and attendants in gold braid. Their elevator has a chandelier in the regency style and music, always music. "Warren cannot tolerate dark, small places," says Mrs. Bidart coming into the foyer. "They make him very insecure."

Like your womb, thinks Maude, and yet he's sorry he was ever born. Maude cannot tolerate Mrs. Bidart, who is wearing a new fur — lambskin dyed cobalt — and cowboy boots with spurs. If there were any justice in the world, Mrs. Bidart would be behind bars for begetting this boy, a child discarded like a blouse that didn't work out.

"Where's Warren?" asks Maude. He lay there in his expensive snowsuit, hidden from the world. "Oh, there's a package at my door," says Maude, bending to the child, poking and prodding, "a fat, soft package." One eye appears, then two, then the whole clever face of Warren Bidart giggling, bubbles of spittle at the corners of his angelic mouth, like any three-year-old. "A package to open," says Maude.

"That floor is filthy," says Warren's mother. She doesn't give a damn if the snowsuit is dirty, nor the child's cashmere scarf and hat. She hates Maude Lasser's playful moments with her son. They were only moments to be sure, flashes of normalcy before he turned into the monster she lives with. She hates the early morning trip across town in a taxi. And the woman will not let her send him with Inez. There were doctors in their building, Moe said, but she said the shame of it. Her kid doesn't need a doctor, but the nursery schools where Warren would not talk or play, where he sat picking at his legs and arms until they were bloody, said the Bidarts better get someone quick. Lois Bidart hates her son's therapist, an aging woman with gray hair any which way and awful clothes, the worst run-down heels, blunt fingernails, wrinkles — on her upper lip, a few coarse menopausal hairs — and yet she was pretty. Lois Bidart hates that: this rag-and-bone woman is attractive. Maude looks at Warren pulling off his hat and mittens, looks at the child steadily with bright interest as though she cared.

She cares for the check at the end of the week, thinks

Mrs. Bidart. And what was she to do for fifty minutes while Warren goes off and says God knows what to the woman. The boy never speaks to *her*. What was she to do sitting here every morning in this hideous hall. She hates the worn rug and the pieces of cracked china that hang on the wall, mended plates with the same old bridge, tree, house blurred with age. She hates the empty vase the color of blood dried under Warren's fingernails after he's had a long scratch. From her purse, a loose sack of gray lizard skin, she takes out a mirror, a tweezer, face cream, pills, two books: *Woman's Body: An Owner's Manual* and a romance. Tweezing, creaming, flipping the pages — what the hell was she to do for fifty minutes. Next week she will send him with Inez. "Urine is normally straw- or amber-colored. . . . Only in very exceptional cases do women lose all their hair. . . . A nail consists of a small plate of dead cells." Mrs. Bidart takes a pill without water, swallows it dry rather than going into that nasty bathroom with the broken tiles and pictures of Gilbert Lasser shaking hands with Lyndon Johnson and Vladimir Horowitz; the sink pitted — so old — and the paint worn off the toilet seat. Mrs. Bidart reads:

> Gwynneth, Lady Elsmoor, waited for her heart to stop its violent beating. A flush stole down her jeweled throat, across the ivory mounds of her heaving breasts. Never had she been more alluring, more alive than she was now in the loathing of this man who faced her, a common man smelling of stables and sweat. William Bliss had known her as poor Gwynneth Leeds and it was to this creature she had given the bitter joy of her maidenhead.

The basket intended for firewood holds plastic and wooden toys, stuffed animals. Maude Lasser's patients are mostly children. During the past few days there had been some indication on Warren's part that he might like to play. He had spun the tire of a dump truck obsessively while Maude talked to him. Sucking his thumb, he had pried the frog's eye off a bean bag. She has written *increased affect* in his file. Now his attention wanders from the manipulation of his almost perfect silence.

"Botto," he says.

"What's botto?" Maude asks.

"That man is botto," says Warren. It is all guesswork, but Maude draws a silver spaceman out of the basket and places it beside the boy. Warren turns away. In his file she writes *botto*. She is keeping a list of Warren's words, the language he substitutes for the one he will not speak. Remarkable progress — twenty nouns, eight verbs. Brilliant. He had not spoken for weeks when he first came to Maude at Christmas, a delicate boy not of this world, buttoned like a ventriloquist's dummy into a miniature polo coat. She remembers how mechanical he was taking off his English cap and little leather gloves and how he crawled up on the couch and rolled there with a vengeance so that she might see, under the disarray of his shirt and knee socks, his remarkable wounds. Round holes as though scattered buckshot had hit his legs and arms. Working hard and late the child had pierced his flesh: some lesions were scabbed and others bore the inflamed red ring of infection. Tumbling on the couch, he looked triumphant.

"We have a salve," said Mrs. Bidart. She sat in Maude's office sweltering in a mink cape with Mr. Bidart at her side. He was bloated with prosperity, twenty years older. Moses Bidart had a first wife on Long Island, North Shore, grown children. (Maude made notes.) Now he had sex, Lois, the East Side apartment and this pitiful child of his late flowering. Warren beat his head rhythmically against the arm of the couch, a relatively harmless performance for the three adults.

"I'm in graphics," said Mrs. Bidart. "How can I work? I'm upset." She flipped her hand at Warren. It seemed an unusable hand, with long lacquered nails clawing the air and a diamond, comically large, weighting it down.

"I'm not right for you," Maude had told them. They needed a fully trained psychiatrist with the best diagnostic skills.

"It's a stage," said Mr. Bidart. That was a statement of fact and Mrs. Lasser with her Ph.D. and certificates on the wall better believe it. The ape, Maude thought, for that's what he looked like, with a great expanse of stomach and his head drawn down to hunched shoulders. He would never admit failure — and there was Warren, the loss, a dainty boy locked in his silent pursuit of self-destruction. Defiantly Maude took him on, confessing to Bert that it was unprofessional, but it was either her attempt at treatment or an institution for the boy, surely. The Bidarts wanted to get on with the unsatisfactory pleasures of their lives.

Progress: Warren plays peekaboo like a baby; Warren talks. He wanders around Maude's office each morning giving names to objects — botto, mok, rellido — all set in perfect grammatical sentences. Each day she marvels at the energy and intelligence he devotes to his sickness. Lately he turns from wherever he stands in the small room and without facial expression touches Maude's skirt, her sleeve. She must always be there. On Fridays he is distraught, knowing he will not come to her for two days, dreading a slight pain akin to loneliness. One day when Maude was not well he followed her to the bathroom and batted his head against the door. "I'm here," she cried out from the toilet. "Here I am, Warren." He does not feel the bruises and lumps he inflicts on himself or the holes poked into his flesh. She can only imagine how often he was abandoned by Lois; left to idle in his crib; left to the boredom of his magnificent toys; verbally, most likely physically, abused.

"Pana thay," Warren says, holding her sweater. That means they are to read.

It is indeed a day of progress, for as they sit down the boy grabs at a picture book: "I like this one about the cow," he says. And they both laugh at his plain English. It is a folktale he likes with peasants and a magic cow levitating in the starry night. Then he shows where he has gouged himself raw on the arm, though all the rest of the marks are healed into dull purple scars. Just this one new place.

"Does it hurt?" Maude asks.

Warren does not answer but he begins to cry. Methodically, he cries for forty minutes in Maude's lap. As though he knows when the appointment is up, the time his father pays for, the boy gathers himself together. "Okay," he says and walks out to the hall.

"Warren spoke so nicely —"

"He doesn't speak at home," says Mrs. Bidart. She packs up her makeup and books, then watches her son, who slowly gets into his snowsuit for the taxi ride home. Furious, Warren's mother asks, "Why was he crying?"

The patch of dark sky Maude can make out over the courtyard is ominous as she listens to this week's story from a family who have betrayed their little girl with a new baby. Attuned to every nuance of the child's "hostile" behavior, they spout demotic Freud. She makes notes on how to terminate the case, but fears they will wander from one therapist to another looking for preventive medicine — with some anxiety but no symptoms.

By the time Ana Lopez arrives at the door there is a dusting of snow on her shoulders; snow is melting on her slick black hair. Ana is with the City Ballet, troubled since high school by her success, guilty that she was not watching morning television and drinking beer on Amsterdam Avenue with the rest of the women in her family. Now she is going on tour with the company and will not see Maude for six weeks.

"Let's make coffee," Ana says. She wanders free in the Lassers' apartment, pretending an innocent game, that a woman like Maude is her mother and some man like Gilbert Lasser whose name she has read in the paper . . . Maude allows this: she does not think she will see the girl again, except on stage or perhaps to take her to supper after a performance. She will miss watching her move with grace around the kitchen and sit with her professional posture on the edge of a chair. She will miss the exotic look of the girl in black leotards and jersey skirts, the purity of her neck. Always a bit onstage; Ana's discipline is wonderful to behold, the dedication in each gesture. Tightness has turned to containment and there is a sensuality that's new, a fullness of spirit that might one day come through in her work. Maude cannot guess if she will be a great dancer. She knows that Ana is being courted, somewhat formally, by an intern at Mount Sinai, that Balanchine has chosen her to dance Calliope, one of the graces in *Apollo,* while she is on tour. Ana Lopez will never again live with the interminable high-pitched jabber and cha-cha music in her mother's house. She pays dearly to come to Maude and for a clean studio apartment, but until recently she was not sure that this is her real life, not a hoax. Now that she feels entitled to her peace, her work, she no longer has time for a therapist or the need of one. Nothing is definite: what remains to be seen in Maude's view is whether the quiet place, the young doctor, and a principal role will always seem thin compared to the excessive emotion and survival tactics of Amsterdam Avenue. For the next six weeks Ana's course is set. She dries Maude's cups and saucers while they discuss durable suitcases, plane tickets, the bitter cold she dreads in Chicago. Everything in place, Maude says, "Thank you."

"Well, I never could stay still."

They go to the hall, where after a false theatrical kiss they stand in place for a moment before the next movement.

"Good-bye," says Ana.

"Standing ovation," says Maude, just that phrase, and closes the door.

The answering machine on the desk tells her who has called during the morning. She keeps track of every hour meticulously, as though to make up for lost time. The sound of her voice like the voice of a chirping, much younger woman says, "I am not available at present." It is a voice with no depth, with a lilt intended for platitudes or cheerful simplification. Bert agrees that we do not like to hear ourselves recorded, our words stolen, the spirit sucked out of us, liable to distortion. The voice says: "I will be *glad* to call back."

But this noon there is no one to call. A meeting at Columbia is canceled. Elizabeth is at a pay phone on Broadway with wet feet, asking if there are any extra boots or her old shoes in the closet. The mother of this afternoon's anorexic patient cancels. The day has changed. This morning has gone by without her knowing . . . and she takes herself to the bedroom almost at a trot. The sky, white and sunless, is seen through a bluster of snow against the windows. Snow is piling on the window ledge and has stuck to the scrubby winter lawn in Riverside Park, drifting against benches and trash cans and up against the battered retaining walls of the highway. New Jersey is a blur of romantic palisades planted under the dull new building-blocks of Fort Lee. The river is black, dead black: the set from her window has changed; so have the directions for the afternoon, and as Maude settles into the creaking wicker chair, the morning with news and coffee seems as remote as a summer holiday. Where were those people sailing down the cold rim of the continent in their bright vacation clothes? And why does she think of them first, lying nauseous in their cabins off the wetlands of New Jersey — and not of Elizabeth pregnant with wet feet?

It's 12:30. The phone has let her down, the weather, too. She has journals to read, notes to write up on Warren — his language and what must be seen as a remarkable breakthrough, his tears. On the shelf in her closet she keeps a quilt started for her grandchild: this is to prove to herself she can slow down and do it — the long and loving domestic chore. It is not art but a sentimental craft. The pieces when stitched together will form a central star — what is taken to be a star, pointed and perfectly symmetrical. Scraps of Elizabeth's baby dresses, old aprons, Gilbert's custom-made English shirts that have gone at the elbow. He calls it idiot work. She agrees, says it's just the beginning of her cottage industries: she'll bake carrot cake and weave lumpy rugs right here on Riverside Drive. He has the good grace to let Maude waste her time with the quilt in the hour before bed; she sews poorly.

On the West Side Highway the cars move hardly at all. A man walking below bends into the wind, arms flailing against the elements, comical in his plight like a dark reeling figure in a silent movie. An Act of God, she calls the storm, though strictly speaking it's predictable. She sits, holding the morning paper. There is the picture of the male gypsy moth in flight and another of a tree trunk with the eggs preserved in ingenious brown crusts for the next year's destruction. No picture can show what she remembers. It was the year her mother died — another Act of God.

Maude had first noticed it on a Tuesday. The weak maple tree that was very old shivered in the sun as she backed down the drive. Its leaves were pierced with pinholes, and invisible strings dangled a few pale brown worms onto the hood of her car. The season was so advanced as she drove the miles south toward Long Island Sound that when she parked in the lot below her mother's apartment the trees spun a dozen larger, darker worms onto her windshield at once; the leaves were shredded fernlike to the spine.

"Stand still," said Belle Petry, "you got one in your hair."

"She has head lice," said Veronica Fain. "Why not say it? She picks them up at school." Off she went for the green soap and fine-tooth comb she would not find in that apartment. Her mother was right: Maude had once had cooties, miraculously small and white, all over her scalp — picked up from the poor kids down the block. Her mother had kept her home from school, washing her head repeatedly with water so hot that she wept. Allowed up for air, the little girl saw that they both were weeping. For her mother it was the shame. At the time of the gypsy moth, Maude Dowd was a widow, but she sat up on a stool like a child while Belle picked four or five worms out of her hair.

"Last night," Belle reported, "she put on the old fur coat and got ready for church. That was about two. By four o'clock she'd opened three cans of chicken noodle soup."

"I know," Maude said, meaning she knew the unpredictable turns of her mother's madness, meaning she knew Belle was vigilant and kind beyond the call of duty.

"No, you don't know," said the nurse. She was all dressed up (Maude remembers Belle on their last excursion) in a red print suit with frilled collar and a string of old glass beads shimmering. "But you are going to know." At an exorbitant price they got the superintendent's wife to look after Mrs. Fain. They ate char-broiled steaks in the garish Tudor restaurant of a motel by the turnpike, Belle Petry drinking sweet manhattans, smoking stylishly. "Now you listen," she said to Maude. "Coming and going you don't see, but all spring there's been slippage. A time comes."

"Oh no, her heart's strong, and that energy," Maude said, "watering plants in the middle of the night. Defrosting the refrigerator at dawn."

"A time comes," said Belle. "She's tired of it." And Maude thought what an odd business; the prediction of the old nurse was classical. She could not see through the amber bull's-eye plastic of the taproom window to the day beyond. It was early June, 1971. Worms curled like pellets in a fold of leather on Maude's purse.

Belle said: "It was maternity they all wanted; any hospital I worked at, that was the attraction — handling the babies, or the pediatric ward. But I wanted the dying — folks on their way out. It's a lot of care but it's interesting, a life at the end. Not old people lingering in a home, but the dying, some of them fighting, but mostly easing out — that's the way. Your mother's been busy, we know, but now she lets go often and lies there, lets it drain from her. I have always enjoyed attending to death, normal death."

"When?" Maude asked.

"Soon, I imagine." Belle read over the dessert list but was not tempted. The years of keeping her figure had set her ways.

"I wish you had known her," Maude said and presented Veronica Fain in eulogy . . . her mother generous and sane, good times in the old house, a handsome woman, too, well read. It was a dull picture. "She made a chocolate cake like a log cabin for Lincoln's Birthday and invited the neighborhood kids in. . . ."

"Is that so," said Belle. She ordered brandy with her coffee and the waitress, a snit of a girl, winked at Maude. The attempted worldliness of the restaurant — the dimmed lights, the stained red carpeting, an instructive wine list — this was the old girl's milieu: a little peace after the hospital duty, a little glitz, a drink with a man across the table — for Maude knew there had been men, that the late marriage to Dr. Perty came after Hubie and Stan, after Claude (married with kids), after the big insurance salesman. Veronica Fain with the grand house, her father's house, driving out to the garden club, the League of Women Voters, the antiques fairs, would not have been Belle Petry's friend.

"My mother painted murals in the cellar," Maude said. "Red Riding Hood. Boy Blue. My mother made flower arrangements, mostly Japanese."

"Is that so." And then Belle, placing her hand flat upon her heart as though she was about to pledge allegiance to the flag, said she had an aneurism, repeating it — an aneurism — for some time known. A matter of life and death, weakening of the vessel. There was little chance of surviving the operation at her age, but what the hell.

"No," said Maude.

"Well yes, honey, and you had better find another nurse. They can take me at Saint Vincent's next Thursday, bright and early."

They had gone shopping for nightgowns and talcum powder — all the paraphernalia to pack for the hospital — as though it were a short holiday, Belle choosing carefully the shade of pink in a quilted bed-jacket, just that soft color of a Betty Prior rose that became her. The Doctor had maintained a rose garden in Florida. "The one thing I hold against that man is how quick he went. I didn't properly see him out."

They sat in the car watching the trees sticky with larvae, the worms dancing down to them. "And one more thing." This is what Belle set herself to say — Maude understood that from the clear gaze of the old woman, understood it still as she stared into a blizzard on Riverside Drive. "You don't ever settle — driving up and down. You don't look at me or at your mother. You live for no one — certainly not that big lump of a girl. Do you think it's all errands and daydreams?"

"Yes." Maude replied like a child and gave the weak excuse that her husband was dead.

"Nonsense," Belle told her. "I've had lives, and then lives . . . not the worst of which was my survival here, tending to your mother."

Upstairs, Mrs. Fain tattled to the superintendent's wife . . . that fine lady smoking, and her daughter had ringworm on her hip — Maude, who came here prim and disapproving, dying of slight agony or shame — and had trench mouth, too, when just a girl, her gums and lips had to be painted with gentian violet. Maude brought home every disease from those poor children down the block.

That day she had not driven home on the back roads but went directly, on the highway. She had not stopped at Regina Caeli to see Paul Deems. Deaths, plural — the prediction was sobering and Maude did not want to flirt or buy his favors. For weeks she had been sleeping with him, an urgent affair. When the excitement of her hot pursuit was over she found the actual arrangements to be reasonable. His phone calls came after his wife slept. They met in Danbury at ethnic restaurants of no distinction, then drove on to one of the motels that clustered about the entrance to the Interstate. In these bland rented rooms they fell upon each other in a fever of passion. Next they plotted to make sure Elizabeth was not at home: finally behaving like a normal kid, she had taken a role in the school play. On the sofa bed of a dim and neglected "study" in Maude's house they lay in rapture — Monday, Wednesday, Friday. It was fair given her loneliness and his deprivation that they should claim each other. She undressed in haste and waited for him, one arm across her breasts, the other held down to cover the bristly auburn hair of her mons veneris in a show of modesty while she waited for him to stand naked above her with a prick that was erect. What she remembers clearly is their language, that they had said *clit* and *cock* to each other as though they had reinvented the words and tinged them with soft-focus notions. *Cunt,* they whispered, *cunt* and they had fucked but their performance was lost to her now. On the sofa bed they had fucked and called it that repeatedly: she had thought the word romantic. In retrospect, it was the kind of fucking and screwing so set against the world, the kind of fucking that so excluded the rest of life it was vaguely pornographic. So Belle Petry was wrong: she cared for someone, for this man and for their appointed hours of lust on the sofa bed. Maude Dowd believed she had entered the world again and suspected they knew in the market, in the Post Office. Mattie Le Doux, in particular, she avoided. The surviving Le Doux sister in spectacular mourning wore a black straw boater on her copper head and shiny sacks of black jersey adorned with costume jewelry. Maude felt the woman smirked at her and she expected Mattie to appear on that disreputable back porch exactly when Paul Deems arrived to hide his car behind the closed door of her barn.

In love, she started when she saw him, wired for his slightest touch. In love, she let him talk at her as though from a television screen while she admired his eyes and hair. How striking — the prominent nose. She saw that he was more the man for his peasant shirts, that the strong line of his jaw did not need the reinforcement of a business collar. At fifty he bore no wrinkles, no sign of his suffering. Infatuated, Maude called his face serene. She had given him some peace. With their harmless fucking she believed they had both joined the world. And their future she projected as discreet and tender, waiting for the wife to weaken and die. In the matter of faith she had miscalculated: the religious tone of the gift shop was set by the cripple: her prayers, her politics, her belief.

"I read all those chapters about Philip the Second and the cowardly pope who fled the plague for nothing," she had said.

"I'm sure you improved your mind," said Paul Deems. He had been a three-martini advertising executive and now believed his own salvation was closely connected to the constricted life he must lead with his wife. As it was, he broke the rules Monday, Wednesday, and Friday when he came to Maude. April went by, and May. They fucked, making the word common in their speech. They drank jug wine behind drawn curtains, and at times it was hot in the small room as the season wore on. They exchanged edited versions of personal history, as lovers will. Frank Dowd, dead and gone, was a comfortable ghost: an ambitious and cynical man driven to an early heart attack. His political influence and intricate deals seemed passé as Maude lay with her new man on the sofa bed. There was the smallest whine in her voice to indicate that she had not so much been neglected by her husband as undervalued, while now . . .

Waiting in the wings was the poor wife. They talked of her before and after fucking, wheeling her on stage where she could not come of her own accord. Wasn't it natural that she needed the consolation of faith. Ritual was appropriate to an invalid's life. Paul Deems said she had been a hot number — swimmer, dancer, so they said — but he had known her always in the wheelchair from polio, one of the last victims, so very sweet, with a long skirt over the leg braces, too good for him, untouchable — and with a force of personality she had gained through her misfortune. It seemed to Maude that the woman was with them too often in their room, a presence with her simple name and her open and luminous gaze — that of a saucy college girl in an uncomplicated movie of the 1940s. They talked of her strength and her dependency: Mary Deems was their subject matter.

Wasn't it crazy, they said — knowing it was perfectly logical — that she would be so attracted to radical Catholics, to the most foolhardy priests and nuns who risked their lives crying out against senseless killing. She wrote to these people in prison, long letters of support in an inflamed prose . . . the blood of justice must be shed . . . love each other in these holy crimes . . . as Christ embraced the cross . . . She sent money, which may never have been received, along with her brave words. Each day Mary Deems watched for the mail and was sometimes rewarded with coded letters, which her husband could not decipher. On the refrigerator she taped pictures of her royalty: the Harrisburg Seven, led smiling to the courtroom; a Jesuit defending himself against a billy club with the sign of the cross; a poster of Dan Berrigan's manacled hands set against a ball of flame — "After man understands love, he will, for the second time, have discovered fire."

Twice the FBI had come to the Regina Caeli Gift Shop, and when they saw Mary Deems, wan and pleasant in her wheelchair, pert in her answers to them, she was noted as harmless. Harmless, too, the husband, who was either crafty in his pose of male nurse or actually ignorant about getting information into and out of Danbury State Prison, where Father Berrigan was serving his sentence for conspiracy. And if his wife had anything to do with plots against the government, he didn't know. He shopped, cooked, lifted her from bed to chair, made a living out of bric-a-brac.

On the sofa bed in Maude's house the lovers lay together, their hands caressing one another's thighs, and discussed Mary Deems: in the gift shop they closed the door on their urgent sighs and swift embraces, but here her imprisoned life invaded their pleasures. "She must know," said Maude.

"She suspects I'm not playing tennis," said Deems.

"Tell her," Maude whispered. Unreasonable, in love, she insisted, "You must tell her." She remembers the stale dialogue of their adultery more clearly than their fucking.

But it was the poor wife who conceived a fresh direction: it consumed her: she — *they* must go to South America, to work with the people in Chile or in Guatemala, to save the children, teach the women. Already nuns and priests of the living church — not weak liberals but those who understood that the radical spirit was the only spirit of love — nuns, priests and dedicated lay people were giving themselves to heal, to feed, to teach. Mary Deems received letters from a young Marist brother, a hero in the mountains above Santiago. They must join him in South America: it was the only way to go on living at all. Indian women with sick babies were taped up in place of the antiwar protesters. Life was finished here; as though it was her final comment, she cut out a picture of Julie Nixon Eisenhower giving an engagement present to her sister Tricia — the young matron's favorite recipes in a dear file box, a gift item of such ultimate triviality, which they sold at Regina Caeli. Get rid of the shop and go, said Mary Deems. Go, like early Christians, to fight illiteracy, starvation and disease. She acquired a packet of airline schedules. She studied Spanish. As her husband's affair progressed, she became more vigorous than she had been in many years, as though the miracle might come about and she would stand straight and walk into the world.

"But she'd die," Maude said.

"I can't tell you the medicines she needs," Paul Deems had said, "the care." It would be a form of suicide then — better stay at home and say her prayers.

"She knows about us," said Maude, in anxious repetition. "You must tell her."

On the day that Belle Petry announced her aneurism and the decline of Mrs. Fain, Maude drove home on the highway. She did not want to see her lover in that shop — among the baskets and candles, once vaguely erotic objects, which she now knew by heart — or to draw away from him when customers entered. Death was a serious business. Soon her dutiful trips would be over. And feeling a little grand, a little remote for the awful news, she drove directly home. Deems did not call that night as he usually did, to speak to her softly from the kitchen phone while his wife slept. There was no answer when she called the Regina Caeli — a risk, but she was desperate to hear his voice. She dialed again and again. Well, Mary Deems had made great friends with the local priest; and they went back and forth to dinner with a group of refugees from

Greenwich Village, faded socialists who lived up by Candlewood Lake. The Deemses had a life together, a marriage, and suddenly this enraged Maude, though it was hardly news. When Elizabeth came home at midnight from a rehearsal, she turned against the girl like a madwoman. "Out with those boys until this hour?"

"We went to Dunkin' Donuts" was all that Elizabeth had said.

The next morning Maude bathed and dressed. It was a Wednesday, his day to come to her. She cut the first rambler roses and put them in the study, chilled a bottle of wine, far better than their ordinary fare, bought salted almonds when she went to get the mail. When a teacher from school called to ask if she would sew costumes for the play, Maude said that her mother was dying. She waxed floors, then bathed and dressed again. "She knows," Maude thought, confined to her tawdry lines. "He has told her." She then lay on their sofa bed naked waiting for the thump of her heart to be stopped by the sound of Deems's car, by the rumble of the barn door closing. He did not come. At last, ignoring the danger, she dialed. The phone rang endlessly at the shop, then did not ring at all. Maude dressed. It was 4:15, then 4:30. Belle Petry called to say Mrs. Fain had escaped down to the parking lot to look for her old Chrysler. Trembling by the kitchen phone, Maude did not receive the import of Belle's message.

At 4:50 she went to her car. The light was strangely harsh in the driveway. The house with its red shutters blazing looked raw upon its bed of granite. Small black worms wizened in death lay broadcast on the hood of her car like scattered seed. She drove the back route down to Regina Caeli, the direction she never took. It was unnaturally bright and hot for the season. The windshield, fouled with the bodies of worms, was made worse when she turned on the wipers. Through the stop sign at Lillinonah where the fishermen docked, through the blinker at a high white Congregational church, she drove wildly: all backward from the route she knew, fences and houses on the wrong side of the road, her vision blurred by the slaughter of the gypsy moth — and came to the square of pavement at the doorstep of the shop. A sign read CLOSED. Maude knocked, then beat at the door. She saw shelves cleared, many of the counters covered with old sheets and bedspreads. The lighting fixtures dangled from the wall. Deems is going to paint, she thought, and beat again on the door, then ran to the back of the building, where she had never been. There was a garden — peonies, a deep red; roses tangled over a fence; a cement slope to the kitchen door for the wheelchair; a path that led to one shade tree. But the yard was shocking to her in its unfamiliarity, and inside, when she peered through a window, all was wrong — the place cleared, packed up. None of Mary Deems's causes or mottoes taped on the walls. He is going to paint, she thought again, paint his little house, the bastard, and live on with her in misery. An envelope stuck in the back door read SUBURBAN PROPANE, written so nicely and evenly it might have been penned by a schoolmarm or nun — SUBURBAN PROPANE.

What followed was real, sharply so, as though a film or tissue had been lifted from the day. It remains clear to Maude Lasser: she had rattled the door helplessly and then stood defeated in the garden: there was a faint buzz, rhythmic, inside her skull. A man in a green work suit came into the yard.

"Hello," he said, and he began to detach a silver gas tank from the house. Above the pocket, his shirt read SUBURBAN PROPANE. He placed the tank on a dolly and began to detach its mate. Maude picked up the envelope, which had fallen to the ground, and handed it to him.

He said: "The new owners are putting in electric. They got the best available here" — he cradled the tank in his arms — "the cheapest and best. You're never going to get your low flame on electric. You're never going to get control."

"The shop is closed?" she asked in a voice that was distant and hoarse.

"Sold," the man said. He was a lean old fellow with thick brown skin and craggy features, a cartoon Yankee. She had seen him reading the gas meter in her own yard, placing new tanks by the side porch. They had never spoken. Now she asked him: "Where have they gone? Please, is there anything written . . . ?" and felt that she was crying. She was not.

The forwarding address, when he opened the envelope, was a school in Santiago care of a priest with an Irish name.

"She's a saint," the gasman said. "I'll get my money." He wheeled the tanks off. It was the end of his day, 5:30 by Maude's watch: the end of his purpose, she thought, his entrance and exit. News had arrived in a letter, an efficient plot. She understood that she had been betrayed: Paul Deems had fucked her with the plane tickets in his pocket. "The coward," she said. "The prick." It was like death standing in his yard — what she thought at the time must feel like death. And the little gun on the back road. If she'd bought that gun she could kill herself. The gnawing murmur went on in the stillness: it was the worms devouring what remained. Deserted, she took inventory of the abandoned place — a three-legged outdoor grill rusted among the roses, picnic table of splintered wood strewn with droppings, birdbath split by the frost. Above, the big shade tree eaten to bare winter branches stood naked in the glare-sun, exposing the scene below.

As though to increase her misery, she took in the full extent of devastation on the way home. For the first time she saw that there was a plague on the land. Her own trees were much worse than she had noticed, their skeletal out-of-season stalks were sickly against the white clapboard house. Within the car the caterpillars could be found on her shoulders, her arms, resting lightly on the tip of her shoes, squashed underfoot. A few worms crept along the dashboard; one dangled from the speedometer — full grown it was longer than the rest, hairy and dark with blue and red warts in pairs all up its back.

It was the year of the gypsy moth that she had an idle and disastrous affair with a coward. It was the spring in which she had forced her dreams. Like so much elaborate rhetoric addressed to no one, her fantasies had come to life. So she'd been fucked. It was that year, too, that her mother died, and the nurse, Belle Petry. The old women died in tandem as though they had all along been engaged in a folie à deux. Two caskets. Two funerals. Two graves within a week. Belle went under the knife and Veronica

Fain succumbed on the couch. Mrs. Fain said, "It is my father's couch." She patted the arm — covered in good brown velour to last a lifetime — with such satisfaction, and Maude, who sat facing her, would always say she smiled. Her mother smiled at something private and died, head lolling as though in sleep, but the room in the painful place was noticeably empty of her sorrows and all her fancies gone. The farce of lawyers and funeral directors consoling Maude, twice. Two masses for the dead. Two rides to the defoliated cemetery in black limousines.

At this time, given death and desertion, it had seemed less important, but it was within that month that Elizabeth began to sing. The end of the school year, the final production of the Thespians — a musical, if Maude had been noticing. Miscast as a diminutive Hispanic, costumed in a cocktail dress of pink lace that had seen better days on the gym teacher, Elizabeth Dowd sang. Her voice was raw, untutored. It issued from her large body in lines of pure bleating beauty, songs of amazing innocence and steadfast love. The show was *West Side Story,* an exotic choice for kids who never got to cities, who attended school with two blacks and a family of stray Puerto Ricans from Waterbury. *The world is wild and bright* — tucked under her chin, Elizabeth's little lover swooned up at her. *Only death will part us now,* she sang, managing to get sincerity into the maudlin line as well as doom. It was strangely moving, the kids at the regional high school playing at hatred and desire in Hell's Kitchen. The switchblades and rumbles of fifteen years ago were as distant as the gods at war. Dancing and singing with amateurish energy, they made the shopworn old musical fresh: city people did taunt each other, they believed, kiss and kill and die in the streets as dramatically as this, for love and honor.

It was immediately after the funerals, but before Maude had sorted through her mother's closets and the foot-locker under Belle Petry's bed. She had worn a spring dress with bright flowers, not to impose her mourning on old friends — and accepted a ride up to the high school with the Nyes. But the aura of death was with her as she sat in the auditorium receiving condolences. She remem-bered the look of sorrow on familiar faces, but of pity, too. Unlucky Maude Dowd, lost her husband, now her mother — as though she had mislaid her life. She felt cel-ebrated, horribly so, by her misfortunes, and relief came only when the lights went down, with the first blare of music.

The high-school band was transformed into an orches-tra with the addition of a few squeaky violins for the artistic occasion. The overture — rousing, plaintive — sought her out. She could cry in the dark of the audito-rium: it was all over, her mother's life. The tears that had not come in Saint Michael's Cemetery as she stood at the graveside under blighted trees with an old monsignor (unknown, official) came now. It would take years of work before she understood that she cried that night for herself: she was orphaned. The music bumped with a dance tune and Maude accepted a wad of Kleenex from Clara Nye, in whose kind thoughts Maude appeared to be lucky — free of those trips to the senile mother that drained her, free for her own life and days; she was only forty-three, a widow, a pretty woman. An orphan though. She'd had a father, too, so sadly forgotten by them all, dusted out of her mother's head — that man — along with the years, long years of a steady marriage.

Crying, Maude felt for the first time it was not a blessing, her mother's death. Now she was not Maudie Fain, daughter of Veronica, being read to — stories and poems — or learning to sew, though she would never concentrate on the stitches. In the sun parlor where her mother liked to sit, Maudie aiming to please with needle and thread, and Kevin would come in with a fresh remark on his way to football, baseball, hockey with the big boys. Their mother would blush with pleasure at the sight of him, shameless. Maude had been born to the fact that he was favored, but she no longer had to play the game. Kevin had come to the funeral for two minutes, flying in and out from California in one day, checking the time on his watch, looking old in a suit that was too young for him, skirted and flared. His thick chain bracelet glinted obscenely at the graveside. She could not bear to watch him fuss at the mud on his Italian shoes.

"You ought to come out there, Maudie." No one would ever call her that again. "You come out with Elizabeth now that there's nothing to tie you down." They both knew his invitation to be a formality. She would not go where it was never cold or wet, always sunny and the same, but would live on in the East. That much sense she did have, even then: She would not go to the promised land where Kevin tucked sagging chins and eliminated pouches under eyes during the morning and in the afternoon rode around on a golf cart. She would not go to what he called, repeatedly and infuriatingly, "God's country," where her adored brother, out of Dartmouth College and Yale Medical School, had left his wife and children at the age of fifty for a girl who sewed soft sculptures — dolls, really — that mocked the middle class she sold them to for a wicked price.

At their mother's apartment, Kevin would not touch the food Maude laid out. He ate "different things." It was a plain rebuke. She'd asked her brother if he remembered the murals their mother had painted down in the cellar to cheer them when they played inside on rainy days. But he had no recall of the hollyhocks or haystacks, or Boy Blue or the cows grazing off toward the furnace. And when she'd offered Kevin the German stein, a majolica plate — anything he'd like — the silver teapot, to remember by, he had said: "Charlene has the house all fixed up. You know how women are."

With a thump the orchestra slowed to the lovers' theme. Maude's eyes glistened with her tears, but she smiled at Clara, poked Roger. See — she was all right now. Bango. Bango. The curtain rose on a backdrop of enchanting tenements. Dainty fire escapes had been built by the boys in shop. Lines of wash hung out: "My good pajamas," said Roger, going huffy. "My guest towels," said Maude. And in the alley pristine trash cans, courtesy of Village Hardware. Country boys, greased up, swaggered on stage pushing and shoving mildly, their version of tough. The effort of it all came over Maude — the wispy music teacher, Mr. Mirro, swaying with his baton; the orchestra perched on folding chairs, studious and proud; the Nyes' boy like a bean pole tooting his clarinet. The great effort was tangible, exhilarating. Orphan and widow, she was fine now.

Then the music collapsed, lost whatever simple melody . . . abandoned her. In that awkward break she found the word — *humiliated* by a man. Bango went the drums, whang the cymbals, as though they were out on the athletic field. Dry-eyed, it occurred to her that she had never had any claim on Paul Deems. Even now he must have his eye on a dusky South American beauty, beginning again the display of his passivity, his goodness, his sacrificial role: that compelling story of his need. Maude laughed, she couldn't help it, and saw the Nyes look at her with indulgence. She was all right now, but it was laughable the way Paul Deems made screwing him a pious act. She'd felt like an angel of grace. It was humiliating: widow, orphan, fool. It had all happened to her. Death, deception, the gnawed landscape. All this had happened to her. On stage, street gangs, the Jets and Sharks, exchanged insults in unconvincing New Yorkese. These children had an audience at least for their bumbling melodrama of ill-starred love and rage — emotions they could not possibly understand. Play it out, love and murder, thought Maude; I'm an experienced listener and no better: I have listened to my own voice tell childish tales of back-road adventure, true romance, the mystery of the neighbor house.

"What's next?" Clara Nye asked. The boys' dance had come to an end. They clustered at the edge of the stage, looking to Mr. Mirro in real fear. "What's next?" Maude repeated. What will happen to me next.

Elizabeth sang: that was next. She stood on a rickety

balcony in that terrible pink dress, her face streaked with an orange greasepaint, eyelids splotched blue, and sang as though she'd been on stage for years. Her voice was too large for the auditorium, unmodulated and uneven, but clear, effortless — a magnificent soprano voice. "Tonight" she sang, the banal lyric of the heart's awakening, and there was a murmur in the audience, a hush. By the time *West Side Story* drew to its sentimental finale, Elizabeth Dowd was the local prima donna. Mr. Mirror led her onstage again and again. The audience of parents rose in her honor and Maude, who had gone up to the high school a notably pathetic creature, was the mother of a star.

When she'd told Gilbert of her daughter's artistic "debut" he'd said what a year to revive that upbeat musical, slick version of street-gang fights, while American kids were screaming obscenities on the White House lawn, pissed out of their minds on acid rock. "We were parochial," Maude said, but she could never quite confess her full ignorance to Bert. She had not lived in the world then — Jets and Sharks, her daughter's extraordinary talent — it was all news to her. And the Nyes, who had been so helpful, were now Christmas-card friends. But it was within the year of *West Side Story* that the thin boy with the clarinet, their oldest son, had died in Boulder, Colorado, of booze and drugs, outside a psychedelic bar.

Next, Maude waited for the diagnosis as in a doctor's office, though Bert said it was more like an appraisal. What's it worth? My daughter's voice. A hot vestibule in New Haven with a murky stained-glass window that sealed her in — Maude remembered one oak bench and opera posters from Milan, Vienna, London; dusty dried palms in a cracked umbrella vase. Foreign and peculiar in her dress, Miss Lombardi had met them at the door and taken Elizabeth away at once, as though there were no time to lose. A clotted light came through the window, casting rose and purple blotches on the bare floor, though on the wall a carpet hung, a tattery scrap. Beside her on the bench sat filthy pillows, embroidered in an exuberant peasant design. It was an arty, strange place on a side street near the University. Elizabeth was taken from her without a word. In the distance a sharp thump of piano chords and (presumably) Miss Lombardi's gruff articulation of scales repeated by the girl's sweet voice. Then Elizabeth sang a Puccini aria, painfully memorized, all broken into half-starts and shattered phrases, and Maude was terrified until at last her daughter was allowed to sing it through.

Maude waited, studying a framed announcement of Lilli Lehmann's performance in *Die Walküre,* Covent Garden, May 1884: another world. Next, Miss Lombardi, the first in a long line of teachers, consultants, coaches, appeared with Elizabeth. The voice was fine, not rare as yet, but first-rate. No telling what the girl's range would be. The configuration of the mouth, the broad chest — all excellent. At this point the voice was light, coloratura. Like all the voice teachers they would come to know, Miss Lombardi inclined to grandeur: "It's an exceptional instrument," she said to Elizabeth Dowd in a harsh benediction. "It's a gift."

Next there was a hulking upright piano in Maude's handsome dining room. Sheet music and records littered the harvest table they'd scarcely used. At seven in the morning Elizabeth began her scales, all summer long, and yearned for her lessons with Miss Lombardi. In the afternoons she read biographies of Mary Garden and Nellie Melba. Draped in scarves, beads, and long Indian skirts, Elizabeth postured against the sideboard and strained the dining room with song. With cosmetics and creams stolen from her mother she improved upon her eyes and rather clumsy hands and with her own money purchased *The Harvard Dictionary of Music,* complete. Her talent, her ambition invaded the precisely decorated house. She gave herself to sweeping gestures and dashed theatrically through the trembling rooms. Maude removed delicate prints of fruits and herbs, the dark red vase, saint and geode, all the knickknacks she had bought at Regina Caeli. It was out of her hands.

"Are you all right?" Gilbert Lasser asked on the phone. "Are you still there?"

Maude tucked her needle into the point of a red plaid star. "Oh, it's canceled," she said vaguely, "that meeting was canceled?" He thought she sounded dreamy, not like his wife. She was sewing the quilt for the baby, she said, and he thought it a frivolous project that drew her back to wasteful memories.

"It's all canceled," Bert said with an edge to disturb her reverie. "Kennedy's closed. Have you looked out the window?"

He would be home then at five. And Elizabeth was driving along Broadway for sausage and cheese, jammed behind the wheel of the car, puffy at the ankles, short of breath. She was driving through this storm, a blizzard now. Far from safe, her feet wet and cold. Traffic crept at a dead pace on the West Side Highway, piled up behind the first accident. The city street and park were traditionally beautiful out the window but terribly white and null. They would come home now: Gilbert, Elizabeth and probably Gus, her daughter's husband, whom she did not like. There was not much food in the house and no decent bourbon. Gus made an issue of his bourbon as though he were writing a testimonial for his brand. She came to the end of her stitches and picked up another scrap, tedious work. She had wanted this evening to herself, looked forward to the times when Gilbert went off to save the world — though she loved him, there was never any doubt. It was all canceled: as she poked up and down with her needle she knew it was best — tonight she'd not be allowed to roam the apartment by herself, arranging a shawl to disguise the worn upholstery, fiddling with vases, polishing her mother's butter knives. She had wanted to soak in the tub. Once when Gilbert was away she had lapsed — that seemed the right word — and washed colorless henna into her hair, spent hours primping in the bathroom while cops and robbers played in the background on TV. Drawn to the old ways, though she was foolishly happy, or to some part of herself not put to rest — Maude Dowd — a need in her for idleness, empty hours, the drift.

They would come home: talk and eat. Gilbert would argue with Gus that the licensing of commercial television channels was probably an infringement of the First Amendment or that nation-states had given up on the control of multinational corporations long ago. Something that gently needled. Like a clever cat with a rubber mouse, he'd play with his son-in-law until he got him in the usual corner: Gus had a young man's respect for legal solutions. There was no milk for Elizabeth. After dinner she must go to her office and write up notes on Warren Bidart. He had spoken words. He had cried. While it was fresh in her mind she must get down his way of touching her now, less greedily, the sly smile, his handling of objects. Increase of affect. She would try and make some sense of what she was attempting with the boy, though no one case was like another. Eighty percent of the time her dealing with patients was easy now — the rest remained hell. She would try to find some lesson in Warren's healing wounds.

Wrapped in layers of wool, Elizabeth Muranis sat on the piano bench. She could not, being vastly pregnant, sit in her mother's low easy chairs. The piano keys behind her yelped and rumbled discordantly as she readjusted her sweater and shawl, until she turned as best she could and slammed the lid on them. She never played now, never sang. "Damn, I don't know why I came," she said. "I can't even eat sausage and strong cheese. I get heartburn."

"That will pass," Maude said.

"I thought I came to look at the old neighborhood. The house on Seventy-sixth. Lincoln Center. Carnegie Hall. Remember Selma's studio with the old Beckstein?"

They never spoke of Elizabeth's musical career. Maude was silent, then her daughter said, "I *am* confined," in a soft cry, with her hand upon her stomach. "Perhaps I will feel trapped out there."

But she had made the choice to be a suburban wife, now mother, so Maude said primly: "That will pass, too," which infuriated Elizabeth, who rose from the piano bench and lumbered in her woolly socks across the room to a torn paper bag soggy from the snow.

"I came to bring you this." She waved a piece of yellow cloth above her head, a broad movement she'd studied for the stage, fat goddess claiming victory. Dramatizing now, Wagnerian fury, her voice thundered as she said: "I've brought you my father's shirt. Sew my father's shirt into my child's quilt. The shirt he died in."

Calmly, her mother said: "It won't go. The stars are darker colors, prints and plaids."

"Won't go?" The young woman mocked her mother like a spoiled kid. Once Elizabeth had seemed too old; now, on the verge of motherhood, she seemed ridiculously young, as though she was playing a grown-up role. Won't go? the damn design — it was still something shallow her mother had in mind. The look of things. In an assault on their intimacy, on the good intentions of recent years, she flung the shirt at her mother. It hung like a blotch on the baby quilt in Maude's lap.

"No. It won't go." Maude was angry now as she looked up at her daughter. "It's the shirt they took off him in the hospital. You packed it away in your closet with his wallet, the ring, and the note from that woman he chased. Claire — I never knew her last name. For years. The classical music, really? Frank Dowd? The splendid books they read to each other? Do you believe it?" An ugly laugh broke from her before she cried out. "For years."

"It all happened." Elizabeth, large as she was, could not comfort her mother and gripped Maude sideways. "It all happened. He was my father."

"Indeed he was," said Maude as they held each other in this strange embrace. What good is my training, she thought, the stories I pick at and unfold when I have never sensed that my own daughter has exiled herself to a house and garden in imitation of the ruined past. A house with no piano: she never sings. And there she lives with a corporate lawyer I cannot like, a perfectly amiable, ambitious man, not uninteresting but ruthless, on his way — cutting the depth and shadow out of everything. Elizabeth had married her father.

Mother and daughter: They looked to Gilbert Lasser, as he entered the door, like they were squatting together side by side, facing the camera for a snapshot. Something was wrong, he could see from a distance as he stomped on the hall mat, shook himself like a dog. A neat line of snow on his briefcase slid to the floor. Something was odd. The two women looked damp in the face, red-eyed. It was the inane quilt. Scraps of cloth. An exercise in sentimentality that would mean nothing to the child not born. He was reminded of a tough line from Brecht —"Nostalgia without memory." Clever little German knew what might result from such unhinged emotions.

Mother and daughter: He had met them in a crowded reception room at Carnegie Hall. Maude Dowd, precisely turned out, had looked like a precocious child brought to

the party by Elizabeth, who had a large ungainly beauty
and the powerful chest of an old-time soprano. They were
alert, open to everything, travelers in a new land. He
sensed the pleasure they took in the glasses of cheap wine
that they held, in their shoptalk with young musicians, in
being there. They were living graciously on West
Seventy-sixth Street, just off the park, floor-through of a
townhouse. But they were living like roommates — Elizabeth running to her classes at Juilliard, to her voice coach,
language lessons; the mother doing psychology courses
day and night with the air that she could figure it out.
Learning it all, whatever it was they needed for this life
they wanted dearly. In the city. In the world. To Gilbert
Lasser, who came across them next in the Morgan Library hovering over Mozart manuscripts, the Dowds
seemed like heroines from another time, spirited sisters
from a Jane Austen novel, innocent lively friends from
Henry James, yet they asked nothing special, they were
not precious. He was showing a cultural ambassador from
Ghana around, and tried to explain, as Maude and her
daughter ambled down the gallery of Italian drawings saluting their favorites, that these women were not the
usual, not ordinary, but the man only understood that
they were from a village transported to a town. Yes, but
all the vulgarities of the early seventies — Watergate morality, singles bars, assertiveness training, the triumph of
sit-coms — was a gaudy backdrop in front of which,
happily undistracted, out of whack completely, they pursued their serious affairs.

Elizabeth was working on Mozart arias — Pamina,
Zerlina, Despina, Barbarina — all those ingratiating *ina*s

that were beyond her musically. Maude observed autistic children and gathered data on dyslexia. They'd always just been somewhere — the ballet, the Fulton Fish Market, *Medea* in Chinatown, a morality play at the Cloisters. They'd seen photographs of wrought-iron balustrades in early SoHo. They knew no one except the singers and musicians the girl studied with and a few hungry graduate students Maude had picked up at Columbia. And this mother and daughter were not against things: at the time, he was violent (during panel discussions) on the subject of rackety, mindless popular culture; vehemently opposed to value-free arguments at think tanks; appalled by the corrupt Rotarians who ran and would continue to run the country. The Dowd women were *for* so many things: musicales; something they referred to as good conversation; interesting foreign food; friendships; the arts in general, but with a particular joy in their discovery that modernism blossomed before the First World War. They were for our society, as though it still existed. And then there was their apartment — spacious, personal in its arrangements, as one might imagine an established house in the country: a familiar place to him though he had always lived in cities, in a series of rented walls.

It was nothing that Gilbert Lasser wanted, yet he came when he was asked. "Elizabeth and her friends are singing Bartók." A curiosity: the cold church-hall on a Sunday night, kids singing art songs in shabby formal attire. Curious, too, the scene later in Maude's floor-through, the way people settled in. The safety of these rooms was tangible. It all reminded him of the most hospitable parlors he'd ever known — when, as a student after the war, he'd been invited to the makeshift homes of distinguished scientists, refugees; their welcome had rung true, like this; the talk had been honest, like the Dowds', and somewhat elated. But he could not discover what Maude had fled — other than the disillusion of a suburban marriage ended by her husband's death — to give her this air of survival. The way she leaned into an argument, or gave her attention absolutely to a poor student's woes, or simply held out her hand directly as people came through her door told him she had never expected this time, this reprieve.

He had kept them together in his mind, mother and daughter. It was the only safe way, he'd thought: the mother was pretty with bright auburn hair, his type, the sort of a small-breasted wiry woman he'd always found attractive, but then never got on with because they were anxious, scurrying. Maude Dowd was fatal for him. Self-composed, almost serene as she handed round cake and wine or mulled cider she'd concocted after madrigals. Nothing about her was nervy or absurd. So he'd kept his eye on Elizabeth, her bizarre stature. The oversized nose and chin all in proportion. With her hair piled up and a long skirt she was a classic, the nearly grotesque form of a caryatid on a public building. Her voice was beautiful, indeed. He'd invited them together to lectures and movies as though they were a couple of visitors and he the New Yorker taking them around. It didn't work: his eyes settled on the mother, who looked back at him with that undemanding pleasure of hers in the particular moment, whether they were eating moo goo gai pan or listening to Noam Chomsky.

For weeks he called up women academics whom he'd

"seen" in the past and found them all to be brittle, self-involved, overly ambitious. He had gone so far as to write a letter to his former wife, a chill phantasmagoric creature remarried in Boston, inquiring about their dropout son, sure that this remote gesture would remind him of how inept and careless he'd been in domestic matters. For weeks he knew what was happening to him and tried to forget the color of Maude's eyes — pale green of the sea in direct sun — and to tell himself constantly that she read the most awful books in pursuit of her therapist's badge or whatever it was she'd have at the end of that rainbow. She'd be a disaster informing his friends on the foundation circuit that there was syncopation in cubism or that the opening-night audience rioted at Stravinsky's *Le Sacre du Printemps,* or giving them her thumbnail sketches of Ludwig (she pronounced it *loo,* like a British water closet) Wittgenstein and Ezra Pound. Worse still, the "hostile," "passive-aggressive," "acting out" gibberish that came from her with such girlish authority. But his scorn did not work and he was married to her in less than a year. He succumbed to the cliché that it was natural for his human longings to be irrational: he had never wanted a naive and sincere woman, a high-minded sweetheart, a country girl with gold-red hair — her eyes that clear light green, trained upon the opaque world with expectation. But Maude had been so vivid to him then. She was still — as she stood beside her gigantic married daughter. With her hair cropped, gone mostly white, she was an exquisite lady, though the perfect little figure had gone to scrawn.

"There will be no distribution of the grain," Bert

Lasser said. His trip to Texas was canceled. The little
general, he stood before them drying off his beard with a
foulard handkerchief. "The Portuguese will not eat tacos.
Zambians shall have no cornflakes." Pompous and obvious, he had them laughing at him now. "There will be
no further containment of the cereal leaf beetle. No ba-
gels shipped to Singapore." He marched past them to the
window at a clip. "We're in the grip of a disaster." The
snow fell continuously, a white haze sealing them in. The
snow fell without bluster, evenly, heavily in the dim light
of winter dusk.

Maude came to stand beside him. She could not see
across the street. "It just happened," she said.

Elizabeth said: "What a day to buy sausage and cheese!"

Gus Muranis passed the platter of genoa salami. It was
the kind of meal he hated, cold and unplanned. His
mother-in-law had opened cans of vegetables and made
an indefinite beet-stained salad. There was a loaf of french
bread so small he could palm it. As far as Gus could tell
they were all damn delighted.

"Shipwrecked," his wife said, "and we have to make
the best of it. Find what's edible." Flushed with this adventure: that they were on Riverside Drive without sup-
plies. She was wearing a voluminous striped garment
Gilbert Lasser had brought back from Saudi Arabia when
he was out planting wheat in the desert. Dark braids, still
damp, fell over Elizabeth's shoulders and ended in curls
on each swollen breast. As a rule he took her beauty for
granted, but tonight in that getup as the Amazon Queen
she was spectacular. A gaiety had come over her, a re-

lease that he presumed was the aftermath of her foolish escapade. He had not known she was driving into town until she called from a phone on Broadway, standing out in the storm. Her coat no longer met across her belly. Behind the wheel of their small station wagon she was awkward at best.

The salami and cheese came round again and Gus Muranis scooped up a milky goat cheese: this *chèvre* was finer, he knew, than the greek feta he grew up on, but bland and pasty in his mouth. Of the bread he took more than his share. Maude said they were marooned — that was quite different than shipwrecked. They were safe but limited. She had gone to the next apartment to borrow good bourbon for Gus; there was no milk for Elizabeth.

And Gilbert Lasser, smiling at them, their wise and ruddy little captain, said: "We are only snowbound. Our world hasn't stopped. Consider the possibilities . . ." Gus considered the pale canned pears and stale cookies he got for dessert. He considered Maude, who was so busy with her crazies she could not keep a cupboard stocked. His own mother out in Astoria had a full refrigerator at all times — meat pies, salty olives, aromatic rice rolled up in briny grape leaves. Under the kitchen phone a tin of crumbly sweet *kourambiedes* had been replenished (he believed miraculously) since he was a kid. But his mother-in-law, to be fair, had her crazies to attend. She was onto them now — the successful dancer and a boy who talked nonsense. Gus considered his wife: she was radiant in the candlelight that gave an elegant but farcical tone to this rotten meal. Elizabeth was pleased about something more than the comforting mound of her belly. He considered that his wife had performed this dangerous private act, driving into the city alone. He considered the insurmountable breach between them — his not sensing her mind.

"Take any natural disaster," Bert Lasser said. Now that was what Gus could not tolerate. The way these people talked. Take this. Take that. Considerations. It is not the way we live, Gus thought, questioning if the sun will rise, speculating on the nature of our isolation at the dinner table. There are facts, assumptions as good as facts. Out of a profound silence Gus spoke, out of a sullenness that came from a sense of betrayal — his wife in her confinement had desired Broadway, salami and cheese.

"Take the great dust storms of the thirties," Gus said. "The results were unnatural. The land had been misused. The prairie grass gone. Whole farms were blown under in a morning. The topography of a county changed in one day." Elizabeth looked across to him, shifted her weight. She loved watching his effort as he broke out of his resentment and came back to her. Gus was broad, big, a meat-and-potatoes man. The father of her child. At home she fed him well.

"They had to learn to hold down the soil, to feed it . . ." He was playing their game, pleasing his wife. She reached across to him with a crust she had not eaten. At home Elizabeth would be lying down now on their new sofa while he worked. For a year he had been on the same antitrust case. Ate and slept *United States vs. Amptrex International,* she said, jealous of the hours he spent. Tonight he would have to find an empty corner of the Lassers' apartment. He had corporate records to consider, books of account not yet subpoenaed, hours of it. "In the end they were forced to invent modern farming out there, the most productive land in history, so where's the natural disaster?"

"There was the *wind,*" Maude said. She saw the wind as a cross old man with white billowy whiskers puffing over the Great Plains. "An Act of God."

That was the trouble with the Lassers. They dismissed facts. In any case Gus Muranis's mother-in-law did not favor him. He rose from the table hungry. But Bert, twisting lemon peel into instant espresso, said: "What do you think, Gus? Is the social responsibility of large corporations totally wiped out if liability insurance covers the moral wrongs of directors and officers?"

"Yes," Gus said. He did not want to argue the point, bait thrown out to hook him into one of Lasser's playful seminars where they'd end up with *The Wealth of Nations,* Mr. Justice Holmes, the principles of medieval enclosure. "Sure enough," Gus said. "It's like the erase button on a computer." Then he launched into his routine: it was a parody of the Utah Pie case he'd written for the *Law Revue* at Columbia, and he'd taken to performing bits of it at the Lassers to avoid long circular attacks on the way he made his living. "The major competitive weapon in the pie market was the berry. Respondent's claims were fruitless." Not very funny, he knew: but Gus could make himself a comic figure. A large man, a bulky man, he could turn the corner from handsome to lumpish-absurd. "The impact on apple was negligible, but there remain the consequences on cherry, peach, pumpkin and mince."

Bert, brought down a peg, was laughing. He liked this

straight young man to play the buffoon and remembered himself that very afternoon, strutting across the room for the piteous mother and daughter, vulgarizing his concern. Often, it seemed the only way.

Maude was amused, but she did not like Gus. It was on his account Elizabeth gave up her singing: she believed that against all reason — that he demanded his wife be ordinary, that her daughter's art was sacrificed to a crass man with a corporate image. Nothing was ever said, though her clever remarks on their suburban marriage held the trivial sting of one-liners under *New Yorker* cartoons.

"A night on the town," she said to the young couple, not unkindly, as Elizabeth labored off to her old back bedroom with Gus Muranis in tow.

The snow had built up against Warren's window. It was white but appeared dark as the underside of a thick cloud against the lower pane. There were no sills or trim of any kind on the sleek apartment house, so the snow accumulated magically on the window, suspended in sheets of white twenty floors above Fifth Avenue. Leaning out of his bed Warren could touch the window with one hand. The cold glass. He held his hand there splayed out and brought it back to his face, rubbing his cheeks and nose in a brutal massage. Fully awake, as he often was during the night, he began to rock in his bed, a harsh masturbatory motion that he might keep up for hours, sleeping or waking. The mattress and box springs were strapped and bolted to the floor, like a bunk on a ship, but with persistent rocking Warren had pried his bed loose — partially, so that it gouged the cheap parquet floor in a two-inch track as he rocked urgently back and forth. This sandy, abrasive noise was not heard by Warren's parents, Lois and Moe Bidart, who slept across the hall to the lull of a machine producing white sound so they would not be disturbed by the rhythmic rocking of the child's bed. The grinding of his nights had never been heard by Warren in the ordinary sense.

Slowly, strangely, the snow built on the window, white but dark. He reached out to the cold that enclosed him; suspended him over Fifth Avenue. That night Warren's parents had been forced to stay in: usually the Bidarts went out to eat, often trying a new restaurant, or to a favorite deli on Madison Avenue. Lois Bidart did not cook. She'd had enough of the boy by the time her husband came back from the office. Each evening Warren sat like a little white plaster statue next to Inez, the black maid, who urged him to eat canned soups and sandwiches or the more expensive frozen dinners, which allowed Lois Bidart to say she bought her son the best. Inez had called to say that she was snowed-in at her sister's house in Yonkers, though it was Mr. Bidart's feeling that the Jamaican woman could have made it to the subway but was undependable and lazy like the Puerto Ricans who cut and sewed for him in a loft on Seventh Avenue.

On this night Warren sat flapping his hands and rocking on a Plexiglas stool while his parents ate cocktail tacos and chicken Tetrazzini. Lois Bidart said: "So at least I don't have to drag him across town tomorrow morning." Then the boy went silently to his bedroom, where slowly the snow began to build on the windowpane. He squatted, watching the disappearance of each flake into the mass as he picked at his last scab and dug farther into the soft flesh of his thigh, scraping at the sore until blood began to run down to his sock in a warm stream he did not feel.

When the light in his room was switched on he was discovered to be bleeding freely. His mother, Lois Bidart, said: "Get the salve, Moe." The father said: "He'll lick it off." Moses Bidart, a short, hirsute man of sixty, stood in the doorway wrapped in a red terry-cloth robe shades brighter than the blood that began to congeal under his son's fingernails. A surgical bandage, on hand for these occasions, was applied to the boy's leg and the mother repeated the sentiment that at least she would not have to accompany him to the therapist next day.

Warren lay in his bed until his parents were closed in with their white sound, then got up, closed his own door and removed a night-light from the electric socket by his bed. It was the head of a white plastic duck with a five-watt bulb inside its skull, put there to allay the ordinary childhood fears Warren did not have. Each night the boy pulled the duck's head out, yanking it by the bill. Each morning Inez shoved it back into the socket.

Now it was dim, close. Warren Bidart lay gently rocking, the snow mounting on his window. Each snowflake disappeared into the whole, the darkness building. Now and again he stretched to feel it, spreading his palm (the span of a small page or new maple leaf), rubbing the cold softly now to his cheek. In time the rim of the snow would meet the window blind that hung above. It was almost perfect darkness, soft. The lights of the city below, the massive white contours of Central Park — walls, rocks, trees, humps of benches — could not enter Warren's room. Crawling from his bed, he went to the snow, pressed his hands and whole body against the glass. The imprint of both hands, the fuzz of his flannel pajamas, the mucus from his mouth that wet the window in a kiss was found on the glass. No evidence of tears.

From the warmth of his body, the flat embrace of his body for some extended time, the snow gave way, hurled in one sheet — down. Then there were fragments, without shape, regaining their whiteness in the city light, floating under the streetlamp to bright dissolution. As far as the boy could see. That whiteness, whether a comfort or a terror, now rose to enter his room. Apparently the window of a sleek anodized aluminum had not been locked, and slid up easily for Warren to fall to his death without a word or cry. Light as a spaceman or storybook cow.

Gus Muranis was reading depositions in his mother-in-law's narrow office. An energetic man, he felt that if he breathed deeply and stretched he might push out the walls like a comic-strip hero. How could she stand it, holing up in this cage with the crazies. In an idle moment — Gus had few — he turned through one of Maude's professional journals: one article told of a girl who could not defecate, another of a girl who could not eat. As he turned back to his work, he felt not heroic but put upon — that his wife had engineered the snowbound evening in the bosom of her family.

He had lost hours dawdling at the table in dead-end

Lasser conversation. Then, in the bedroom, Elizabeth had needed him to lie next to her. Reassurance. Forgiveness. It was the pregnancy. His mother had warned him they'd not be running to restaurants and parties. They did little of that. Especially then, his mother had said, a woman gets lonely. It was a solitary project for Elizabeth, he could see, despite the Lamaze classes he went to preparing him for the birth, despite the compassionate vision he had of himself in the delivery room enjoying what would be their mutual elation. "Your father always brought me books," Gus's mother said, meaning magazines. He could see his father in the white canvas apron he wore behind the counter, going next door to the drugstore and buying *Good Housekeeping, Vogue,* titles he could barely read, and bringing them upstairs to occupy his mother while she waited for another child. They lived up over the grocery store in an airy apartment, clean and comfortable. Each kid had a small bedroom. Their father's car, always a Buick from Mr. Pelandrou, sat safely in the garage below.

Constantine Muranis, called Gus, held that his first re-laxed moment in the Lassers' apartment had been when Gilbert said he grew up over the family store — a deli-catessen in Flatbush — only the scene was Jewish. The two men had looked at each other: Bert and Gus, their neighborhood names having stuck forever. Storekeepers' sons. The getting and spending right downstairs, a pros-perity indistinguishable from the good food and the priv-ileged hours awarded to bright boys in which to read, study, play chess.

"Even during the Depression," Bert had said, "it was

a middle-class neighborhood. They bought pastrami, roast beef, potato salad and eventually paid for it." So Gus, as a young law clerk about to marry Elizabeth Dowd, had felt he knew exactly where Gilbert Lasser, whom he'd call his father-in-law, was coming from — or at least where his idealism was coming from. From a boy's world of bookish ideas pursued above the ring of the cash register. Five years ago Bert was rewriting the Constitution and still giving out money to reprint unknown novelists of the Harlem Renaissance. Now he was shifting the face of the earth, which might show quicker results.

The depositions were ones that Gus had taken himself, down in Houston and Atlanta. He read the transcripts over almost fondly, making notes on a legal pad, drawing the facts into a line of reasoning he'd been using on his small corner of the case for months. When they were bought out, Texas Convoy had been doing smart things with computer programs that Amptrex had flubbed. The government was screaming — the old cliché: backward integration. Gus didn't care. He'd constructed an out. At the date of purchase the parent company was fostering internal growth of a parallel nature in Akron and Louisville. He would claim that the defendant was legally safe — Amptrex, supplier and supplied.

Next week he should go to Louisville but might beg off because of Elizabeth and their child. But if he did go — take the limousine to Kennedy, board the plane with his flight bag, sip bourbon while he read Amptrex notes — it would be the last time. The case had been good to him. Gus would be sending junior people who found it boring; he never had. From the beginning his imagination had been caught by the idea of defending an antitrust suit for a corporation grand enough to be a formidable adversary of the United States Department of Justice. It was the heart of American business. The way the world worked. Process. Amptrex was naturally greedy. To build the best case, negotiate with the Attorney General's office, concede, avoid litigation — the law did not crystallize. In his particular and small corner of the enterprise, Gus would come out looking good.

So he sat in Maude's makeshift office at one-thirty, at two — a lone Adonis, oversized, his skin smooth as glossy marble, broad-browed, classic nose unchipped but glowing with light sweat as he worked. *Call Louisville,* he wrote. *Check file on southern acquisitions.* He rose and walked one step to the window, two back. This cell with her crazies, he'd go squirrelly with them: a girl who starved, another who could not shit — though he supposed Maude had no one like that, children mostly, trickles in the vale of tears.

It was twenty after two. He was not tired and thought to go on in the Amptrex maze, except Elizabeth would miss him. She slept lightly now, her distended womb pressing on her bladder. Gus was surprised she had not wandered out to find him — and because he was in this cage for sad children with the chair for them, toys for them, their Kleenex for a cry, he thought how his wife must need him. She had no father. Not a new idea: Bert in his dandified elf's beard, always the intellectual with a general overview of family politics, had never filled the role.

Now that Elizabeth was so big that they could count

the days, she needed him, and at home they lay side by side on their king-size bed, touching her heavy breasts, the nipples grown tender and brown. Together they put their hands upon the taut skin of her stomach, waiting for the churn of life. He would bring her *Vogue* and *Architectural Digest* from Grand Central, buy her any amount of salami and cheese, cancel Louisville. He would catch the early train home each night. So it was nearly three in the morning when he packed up Amptrex and feeling somewhat noble, though without grievance, answered the phone.

It was Maude's line, which rang only here, in her office. Gus said: "Hello."

"Hello," Maude said in a muted ladylike recording. "I am not available at present —"

A woman screamed over the message on the tape, "You killed him" before Gus found the correct button, and then she did not listen, could not hear the replies of a reasonable stranger.

"You killed him. He should have been in an institution. He'd be alive but you treated him normal. You killed a three-year-old child." The woman, Lois Bidart, screamed on — a rasping harangue without pause and without a hitch of sorrow. "I am going to sue for every dollar —" Then Gus Muranis presumed from a guttural male command that the phone was pulled out of her hand.

Snow, a great expanse of it, lined Ninetieth Street. The groan and scrape of the city plow woke Elizabeth. "What's wrong?" she asked. Her husband stood at the window fully clothed, his briefcase with Amptrex papers in hand.

"Nothing," he said. "Go back to sleep." He had decided to wait until morning to report the deranged phone call. What a business: girls who did not eat or shit; his mother-in-law accused of murder in the night. That coarse hysterical voice claiming a child (if there was a child) dead. What a hopeless business. He could not imagine himself chalking up the loss.

The first lone taxi could be seen skidding sideways, turning in from Riverside Drive, then a little brown-and-white dog came prancing on spindle legs in the wake of the plow.

MINOR
CHALAZION

THE WIND that day blew the mosquito netting off the carriage for the second time: an extraordinary English baby carriage, high-sprung with a royal crimson stripe that outlines the chassis. The hood is wicker, padded with a pale pink-gray silk the color of a dove's wing or the translucent flesh of a small cat's ear. Not a realistic carriage, but Gus buys the top of the line. Though it's beautiful, I've never found it useful. We live on a street without sidewalks in a countrified neighborhood of older prosperous commuters who have never given in to paved driveways, streetlamps or fire hydrants. Once I made a fool of myself bumping the baby up and down side roads a mile to the IGA and felt more than ever a misfit in that plain shopping center, cooing at my own child while a crowd of young mothers from the tract houses gathered around attracted by the elegant "pram." As if I was showing off.

The mosquito netting flew across the lawn again and up onto the barberry hedge, was ripped I saw, but methodically I replaced it and sat under the blustering tree with my book. I was not reading. The pages beat against my hand. The sky darkened. Alma, the first hurricane of the season, was predicted. Somewhere a trash can clattered and I heard the slam of a door. When the first raindrops fell they were warm serene splashes on my cheeks, so fat and harmless that I did not save the silk-lined carriage immediately, or my book, but ran for the baby as the netting flew, this time standing with him in my arms, watching the storm come to us. The heavens opened.

I want him to be tough. All summer I had put him out in the sun naked. He was brown and sturdy as he sat on my arm — for he sits up now, nearly. I can see the strength of the lower back over his tight buttocks. I can see his shoulders forming. It rained on us until his black hair stuck to his head in ringlets. My skirt was soaked to my thighs and knees before I rescued the carriage and got us safely inside. I want him to be tough. No calisthenics in the snow. No Bund kiddie swimming in ice water. Not even an American jock playing football or hockey through pain, just tough enough to live in this world. When he was newborn and safely inside, I turned the thermostat down on cold spring days until his fingers and feet were faintly speckled, blue and chill. Often on summer nights I let him swelter in his crib without the air conditioning — when Gus was not home. I have fed this child ground bits of liver, strong cheese, threads of squid and shrimp. He has sucked garlic off my fingers, Lea & Perrins worcestershire, coarse salt.

We've named him Jason. A Greek name that's easy on the modern ear. A prince — I did not look up the legend until I brought him home from the hospital; and though he'll be big, good-looking like his father, even my motherly pride can't project this kid toward the end of the twentieth century holding off mountains, grabbing the

Golden Fleece. Now the name alludes to something studied and forgotten. *Jason* is hopelessly suburban, to use my
mother's favorite slight.

As I am, hopelessly: I wanted this house with thick
plaster walls, copper pipes, an old sun porch, the rooms
large enough for me, for both of us. I wanted the established lawn and full-grown trees. My husband, the choice
son of immigrants, wanted this too. All this — vestibule,
french doors, the breakfast nook, the maid's room — as
though we were about to live as an ideal family before
the Second World War. A life we can only imagine,
American life with nutritious breakfasts and at supper-
time Jell-O for dessert.

I am comfortable in this fixed neighborhood of handsome gray-haired people who drive Mercedes, BMWs,
Peugeots. Gus considers their politics no better, no worse.
Older people. Then, I have never been young. I attribute
this to the death of my father, who went out early in the
arms of his mistress — in the saddle, so to speak (as I
always suspected) — and to my mother's dramatic swing
from frivolity (which I found childish and repellent) to a
high seriousness that overwhelmed me with parental delight. And there was my talent. I sang.

I missed out on giddy friendship. The few nights I
"slept over" with girls it was unnatural to me — all those
secrets, the pointing at cute dresses and shoes in magazines, giggling at articles on vaginitis and the removal of
blackheads, sharing the obligatory joint. At high-school
dances the music was intolerable to me; it seemed trapped
in my head. Amplified beyond endurance. Hick kids with
rude slogans on their T-shirts, tangled flapping hair. I

preferred something earlier — Buddy Holly, Elvis before the Fall, rhythm and blues, something I thought classier — the gentle protest songs of strong women, laments in time of war.

I had grown fast into a woman's body with knockers, tits. "How's your bumps?" the boys asked and it seemed inconsequential parked behind the gym, letting them take off my sweater, plain silly watching them press their mouths to my nipples. Usually stoned, so that to them, to me, my breasts were mammoth contours out there, hallucinations of desire. Their desire. Dummies, I called them. I had that defensive streak from my father, that arrogance of the outsider, which now seems just small-town and cruel. I had simply grown too fast, known death, studied (not hard) and found them — those boys — willful children sucking at my tits, fiddling with the zipper on my jeans. Those boys, I remember clearly. Ben McIntyre with glasses he took off. Lyman Bailey — red hair, air mattress in the VW bus. Wrong to say I've forgotten the dummies — John Meeker, the farmer's son with rough hands, holding my breasts like prize pullets. All of it seldom. Mostly I stayed in my room.

Stayed at home, which is what I should have done that day of the storm. I shut the windows. Dried off. Dressed the baby in overalls and the smallest tennis shoes, as though we were going out. Found my car keys, watch and purse. And while it was still raining, the wind rattling the doors and shutters, I played on my keyboard, the only instrument in this house — not a piano but silent octaves of padded wood on which to practice fingering, a contraption my stepfather bought me not to bother the neighbors on Riverside Drive. While the baby bounced in his chair speaking vowels, I played the Mozart Sonata in E-flat, hearing the notes in my head. Lately I'd done that, practiced — straining over the soundless keyboard through the Chopin and on to easier Bartók pieces. At the end of this repertoire I'd play one song, the accompaniment to an aria or duet that I had studied, while my face reflected the appropriate passions, my mouth always closed.

Alma swept by in half an hour. I took the baby, my things, his things and walked out the front door to see — I suppose the aftermath. A small harmless branch hung off our maple tree. The neighborhood looked disheveled but polite as always, and, strapping the child in, I drove — Gus was off in Washington at the Department of Justice. My mother gone off with Bert to Aspen, a conference on Death and Dying — quite an abstract business as he explains it in terms of "temporal deprivation" and "intelligible catastrophe." I drove north through the ruffled streets — a few blocks up it had not even rained — past a sunny horse-farm and grander houses that are dramatically set in "grounds" behind gates, pretentious and nothing I care for — though my mother thinks I long for luxury, my ease, thinks that I'm now greedy or shallow or both. Because I left the city and I never sing.

I drove north with the baby. He seemed to see everything, sucking the straps that held him, laughing at nothing in particular — wet spots where the storm had been. In my mind there was nothing of a pilgrimage about the trip. I'd often thought to show Gus where I was raised, but I was not misty about the place, cared much less for the New England clapboard of my bleak youth than he did for the ethnic glamour of Muranis Superette. I remembered an awkward house with a steep driveway, decaying barn. I recalled a garish door of stained glass, not leaded, a carpenter's job — and that inside my mother had made the house awfully pretty, which infuriated me in those days.

An hour up, an hour back. In my mind there was nothing of the sentimental journey. I certainly did not intend to drive into the eye of a storm as I had done perversely the week before my boy was born. There was no risk taken, leaving the solid neighborhood I had chosen, we had chosen, to live in. My mother won't get that straight: I did not give up my music for marriage. Gus Muranis never suggested that I go dumb. When we met — in an elevator on the way to Sunday brunch — I fell silent, literally. He was big enough for me. The unmasking: one of those corny recognition scenes — "Ah, it's you. It's *you*," though nothing said. I could not concentrate in rehearsal or remember the words of songs I had worked on for months with Madame Cecchi. I lost four top notes. The lower register, effortless for me always, now had to be forced roughly from my throat. Dumbfounded, I could not conceive myself as any of the great bel canto heroines who proclaim their anguished love in vocal acrobatics. The daring embellishments and inflamed E-flat of Lucia's mad scene that I'd sung in student recitals simply faded.

There was no romantic moor for us, gloomy lake, tombs or noble pride. I was in love with a man from Queens, Constantine Muranis, a young law clerk who was uncomplicated, kind. We slept uptown in his grubby apartment that he'd kept after Columbia Law School, long spring nights of passion that never tired us. There were no melodramatic barriers: Gus was not poor or betrothed to another; I was not consumptive or besmirched. As I walked upper Broadway to meet him I felt it could be seen — that my hips and breasts had achieved a womanly balance from his embrace, that my lips were ripe, split with kissing. Throbbing and creamed with desire, I could have seduced the phone booths and fire hydrants.

Madame Cecchi scolded me — did I think Melba, Mary Garden, Tebaldi threw away their gift for love? I replied that I was hardly a diva and that I would spend my life in minor roles, maidservant or woman-of-the-town, though I knew my voice at that time was first-rate and I'd signed a real contract to go to Santa Fe, not as a student but to understudy. In a workshop production I would get my chance at the lovely aria "Je suis Titania," showpiece of scales and high notes.

Madame said I no longer had purity of tone, that I was incapable of fine workmanship. I said that the sentimentality of *Mignon* was hardly a mirror for my consuming love.

"*This* is the midsummer night's dream!" Madame Cecchi cried out. "This schoolgirl crush." She hoped that my heart would break, this said with heavy sarcasm, so that I might prepare for the more tragic roles, though she knew I was not equipped — a coloratura, *lirico spinto*. She said: "As you are now you can sing on Broadway" (it was the cruelest thing) "with the little microphones flying." But Madame was right. With my shrunken voice I could not have projected beyond the second row. Unprofessionally, I canceled Santa Fe.

She did not come to the wedding but sent a cheap caricature of Caruso that I have never framed. My mother, though she is trained to meddle with the unconscious, insists on blaming Gus. That's the solution for her, but I have no single answer. Passion distracted me; I feared success.

My stepfather came up with the theory that I was nurtured on the extreme plotting of libretti, so that I naturally made a dramatic decision, musically speaking, to go mute. A bit of Grand Opera all my own. There may be some truth in that, in what he says.

Apocalypse across the field, goddamn end of the world. I see so little these days, staying home, and unfortunately it's the distance, the far view that remains sharp while print on the page, the words I live by, contract into a haze. Quite clearly I saw the car parked next door, half an old maple tree crashed over its hood and the windshield shattered to a milky opaque webbing, like a spider's home at dawn. The young woman carrying a baby walked around the site slowly, as though she were in a museum showing the child the ruins of Paestum or markings on an Iroquois canoe, holding the child close up to the crazed glass, squatting with it to feel the bare roots torn from the earth. Pithy roots, that tree's been dying for years. Then she stood awhile in that blank immediate sunshine which can follow storms and I imagine she must have known that big as she was no mortal could shove that hunk of lumber — and to what point? — off the wreck of that car.

So she came loping across the rocky field to my door. I have no neighborly goodwill and curse the remnant of Christian charity that compelled me to let her in. I have no time. Though she was, at first view, a grand figure with her dark hair spilling free, big nose and mouth in the classical style and a calm that seemed remarkable in the face of her disaster.

I let her stand on the stoop with the brown squirming babe, let her presume the place was empty before I flung the door open and said: "I have no time for you." And only then the grand face, almost stupid with composure, did register alarm.

"I'm Elizabeth," she said, but I had not laid eyes on her since she was a fat kid waiting for the school bus. How we do presume our lives have continuity for others. Take for granted recognition — "I'm Elizabeth" — or an open door. Well, I have never let them in here — tax collector, churchy young cousins, alderman, the Board of Health. Soon I intend to oblige them and die. But I will not have them in my house, here where in the poverty of their imaginations they detect squalor, hear rats' claws, see in my shaded windows the reflection of their own dismay and are convinced of the abysmal loneliness within. I have no use for their gothic stories of my dead sister, her festering heart, charred love notes, or of my crimes. The clocks did not stop at some portentous hour when I went mad over a gin bottle or the corpse of an old bouquet. Believe it — Mattie is at work and hears the time tick on.

While the child whined and fretted she stood out there, telling me she was Elizabeth Dowd and never expected that the storm . . . opening her blouse, giving the boy tit, and that softened me, not the mawkish maternal gesture, but the broad sweep of her intent to save them both. Fearless, uninvited, she mounted the last step and I stood back to receive them. The bulk of the two of us in my workroom was tremendous. I am a big woman still. The kitchen is my workroom, the parlor is my workroom, as are the bedrooms above and the pantry rich with mold. All of it laid out to my design, the books and papers not toppling or stray. All as it must be in order to finish. In order. And in each room a place to sit, whether it be straight up at a table or easy in a chair. Well, I admired her nerve looking unfazed at Big Mattie, unflinching like I was no more than herself, Queen of Sheba.

"May I use the phone?" I waited for her to understand from the look of my rooms, from the sanctuary of my books and papers . . . I stood silent as the child dozed at her nipple until she did grasp the idea that there was no phone. Not for years. I had no time, no patience for the ringing.

She said, "The phone was out —" turning to the house she'd come from.

"That's not surprising with a storm, now is it?" And didn't she know, further, that in New England a hurricane come inland could flirt on ahead, then double back to get you.

"I go looking for trouble," she said with a queer smile and plucked the sleeping child from her. Apologetically, she told the boy's name, Jason, and I cleared a place on the floor between the Wordsworthian moral landscapes of the late Depression years and the formal autumn elegy leading to Pearl Harbor, so that she might set him down.

"Walk two miles to town," I said, for I did not like the milky spittle coming from the child's mouth, sucked onto his hands — so near the manuscript. She did not take offense. She did not hesitate, but by the time she buttoned up and slung the boy on her shoulder the sky was dark again. Lightning drawn down to Indian Rock, to the iron ore, lit the narrow view of river and road that has been mine for eighty years. This Elizabeth proceeded boldly — I'll say bravely — to the door.

"That won't be necessary," I said and cleared the unsprung couch of "Night Shift," which treats my war work at the rubber plant in an imagistic prose.

Big Mattie took her in from the storm. Standing order for the groceries: I've maintained my size, though I am blanched — skin white, lips white, hair the yellow dinge of white that never sees the light of day. Inside always, I dress in the old clothes, rowdy as I always like them. I affix a scarf or flower, some pasty glitter. On slow days I change the thick strands of beads from jet to coral or pearls that hide my gobbler throat. It takes little time. It is myself. Big Mattie took her in from the storm.

She said: "You don't have much company."

So it began, our social encounter. No lights — well, that's been a while, but the candle stubs, cold food, canned milk. Years of work shifted from tables, and "The Armistice Ode" from its spot by the sink. I was glad that child could not yet walk, do his harm. After a silence I said: "No visitors allowed." I'd lost the back and forth of it, ordinary speech. There was no need. No time.

Speaking, I tried to get the knack of it: "How is your mother? Though I do not care. Always an empty woman. Pretty, if peahens are pretty. Read too much with little understanding. Always a lazy woman prying into the pitiable affairs of Jane Le Doux, into the ribald affairs of Mattie Le Doux. Never learned a lesson. With field glasses like a commie spy, plotting her trashy mystery — though we were soon enough abandoned for the fellow who came to screw her afternoons. *Lovers swear more performance than they're able.* Hers was a sordid farce, him slipping out the driveway as you were shuffling down the road from the school bus. Three sets have lived in that house since. Weekend people with no taproots, like the old boyfriends beyond. Pretty — they're making the countryside pretty, dredging for duck ponds, extending the flower beds, renewing the spent New England soil. When they dig us out they'll find that after the apes, after the Indians, the settlers, the tradesmen and farmers — the weekenders came to make it pretty. How is your mother? She had the looks in her small way, but she was inquisitive and idle."

Lost the knack; she was sobbing and that started the child off, too. "My mother works," she wailed. And after much fuss with the blouse and nipple, "My mother helps people."

She was at the door, all for walking out to hail a car on the road, but I told her not with the wires down, trees down. The river flooded at the bridge. But she was look-

ing for trouble and in my social way I said: "Stay, uninvited. I make no apologies — it has been years since I
believed that it *is enough to stop in company with the rest at
evening.*" And I asked: "How is your mother? Being a
nice bit of fluff, did she get herself a man?"

"My mother remarried," Elizabeth said, sniveling.

"That would be right, remarried and snug. *I took my
fun where I found it,* but I was never up to entertaining a
gentleman in my home for an hour, a quick shot. Oh,
not lady enough for that. I'd rather the honesty of the
bars and bushes. But what a slick man he was, the afternoon caller came to Maude Dowd. You did know he
murdered his wife. With finesse. Took her to the Andes
in a wheelchair. Took her to the steaming jungles fetid
with tropical disease. The wife was teaching women and
children hygiene and the alphabet when he went off with
her medicines. There were inquiries. It is years since I
have read a newspaper but I saw in *The Advertiser* they
throw on this stoop — he's back in business. I was truly
amazed at the announcement: Paul Deems. Vitamins.
Whole Grains and Honey . . . down on the back road to
Easton . . . All that's Natural. Free to put his hand up
any housewife's skirt. County cocksman. I presume they
are attracted by his infamy as well as the kisses and en-
dearments. Women love a celebrated man. I'd think your
mother might come back here, not you, to her bower of
bliss."

"I didn't 'come back' " — the young woman spat this
at me before the waterworks started again. "I was curious."

"Like your mother, a curious woman, a conversational

woman. That was never my bent and now I've lost the art of it completely. Oh, I loved talk with beer, with a man. I could talk a prick stiff without a helping hand, ancient plaudits as to knob and length — softly mouthing the words of my own prodigious depth and muscular control was magic, incantation riddled with cliché . . . *for I am sick of love.*"

"If I could put the baby down . . . ," she said. Conventional fear had composed her weeping face. If she was to be a prisoner for the night, then at least the child . . . The amount of time they took. To me the unspeakable pain of accommodation, lifting the "Elegy for President Wilson" and "Bawdy Ballads of the Jazz Age" off my sister's narrow bed. Wash? There's a well but no water with the pump gone. Swaddle the boy in rags. Pull the chain — if you must, an empty gesture. Blow out the candle. In the dark I asked her, being sociable — "There was, as I recall, some reason why you went away?"

"Yes," she said wearily. "I sang."

I lay rigid on the bed all night, my right arm stretched out around Jason, who turned and moaned in his sleep. I felt he must know he was not safe at home in his crib with the hideous quilt my mother made. The air was heavy and stale. I rose to open the window but it was permanently nailed or swollen shut; then I lay with him again, rigid. The whole night I turned only to comfort him with my breast so that he would not cry.

For a while I heard her wandering in the dark and lines spoken, her hard old voice repeating lines rhythmically — the words I could not hear. Finally there was the thud of her body, the squeal of bedsprings and a blessed silence. She is depraved, I told myself, quite crazy, with a foul mouth. Uncivilized. And I tried to remember the two old ladies who lived across the field, New England eccentrics: one of them fat and scandalous, the other a colorless twit, poet of small fame, laughed at in this town. The harmless Le Doux. My mother had taken an interest, was indeed curious and at that time she was idle, but the rest . . . Oh, my maligned mother should come back to our house as it is now. There is no sign of her foolishness or of mine. There is none of that jaunty decoration of rooms that covered the dullness of her ungrieving heart. Not a garland, not a brass sidelight or Victorian plant stand remained. I shoved my way through a front door, which, when I forgot my key, in the old days, had reliably given in. Walls had been knocked down and the parlor stood open to the hall. The house was not cramped as I remembered it. A sewing machine faced the porch and there was a dress half-stitched from a pattern that read MISSES CLASSIC SHIRTWAIST WITH SLEEVE VARIATIONS. Of a discreet brown wool that told me nothing. Upstairs in *my* room, a boy had hung his hockey pads and helmet. Under a picture of a rock star with bloody slashes painted on his chest, an array of fragile beetles and moths were pinned to wooden blocks or rested on snowy cotton mats. The place smelled heady with formaldehyde and sweat. The rooms were plain and each one contained an amateurish piece of homemade furniture stained and heavily shellacked in what I took to be the father's chalet style. My mother as she is now would like these people, their pursuits. While I wandered their house I heard thunder but never understood that the storm had begun its violent reprise.

So that later I lay like a charity case on a madwoman's bed. At the first pale light I got up, thankful that the baby slept. He had worn himself out with crying at unknown hours in the night, as though he understood this place to be worse than anything I'd provided — the heat or cold — to toughen him up. Mattie Le Doux was out of my range. It was a matter of hours till my release. I would walk to a phone, rent a car, be home before Gus. Safe in our own sound house it would be easy to confess the bizarre turn my innocent drive had taken. Only then would I sense the danger and grieve for the loss of the car.

Papers were littered by the bed — cheap paper like newsprint that scattered underfoot and crumbled in my hand. Line after line of an untidy scrawl, a word blanked out, additions sliding off the page, but all of it quite open and legible:

> *And at Versailles your spectacles*
> *Blind with sun reflect*
> *Bright vacant days of adulation:*
> *Foreign work undone. Undone our innocence*
> *Before you see the smiling photos sickly dull,*
> *Discredited beside the sharp cartoon*
> *"Veelson" tottering, top hat and spats,*
> *Costumed for a century gone by.*

The script was unorthodox but round and clear. Each capital, a lunatic invention, lawless *t*'s, flighty loops of *y* and *g*. The poem — for that is what I took it to be —

described the downfall of the League of Nations. Unfortunately, I know more about the Flemish alliance in *Don Carlos* and the politics of the gods in *Dido and Aeneas* than I do about modern history, so I cannot judge what seems to me a bitter view:

> *We would live on in tampered twilight —*
> *The novelty of neon haze.*

Passages from a personal life were interwoven with elections, anarchist strife, baseball scores: a country girl, long since "deflowered," seeks the pleasure of dance halls and summer resorts, gorging on song and food, on sex. A story so lewd, so terribly . . . but precise. "Stockings rolled beneath her buttocks knees . . . red hair cropped, ashine with brilliantine." "Big Molly" straddling soldiers beneath the boardwalk, naked thighs stuck to rumble seats, bare fanny pricked with dusty plush in movie shows. That is what she calls herself, "Big Molly," and if there was a blush left in me it came then, at the accuracy of her recall — the place, the year — with all those men. By this time I was no fool and knew Mattie Le Doux wrote all these scribbled pages flaking at my touch, wrote . . . the whole house full. Then I remembered the note my mother had received from Jane Le Doux at the time of my father's death, a simpleton's note in a perfectly even hand.

When the baby stirred I put him directly to my breast and stole downstairs, tired and cold but no longer afraid. In the calm light of day the hall and kitchen were cluttered with papers, all there was of a life. Here was a mystery, complex to the point of absurdity, silly as any light opera I had ever sung. On the back door a crumpled paper bad read

For this losing is true dying;
This is lordly man's down-lying,
This his slow but sure reclining,
Star by star his world resigning.

"Not my words," said Mattie Le Doux. "Thank Mr. Emerson for the gloom and wasn't he clever to figure it out. It will be no pity when they dig us in. Now's the hard part, without time. I haven't the days left, so you can see how troublesome it's been having you here with that child crying and sucking. You thought to get out before Mattie caught you. No chance. I could hear you up there breathing on the pages, touching them when the light allowed. Nose trouble, like your mother. You can tell her now what she nearly guessed. It was Mattie wrote the poems, not Jane Le Doux. Mattie had the way with words, the way with men. It's not given out equal, you know, like presents under the tree. I had it all — the sex, my art."

"Please," Elizabeth said. The baby was fretful, allowed her no freedom of motion while Mattie maneuvered in front of them to bar the door, her face a mask of madness and age, floured white, dabbed red at the lips. She was costumed this early in black and white, a ruff at her neck. Elizabeth had seen *Pagliacci* with just such a sad fat clown. Neutered, Elizabeth thought, powerless, but then she saw the cast-iron pan Mattie Le Doux held as a weapon and recalled murder on stage, the famous tears.

"Promiscuous," Mattie hissed at her, "but my art, I kept it pure. Unsullied with talk and public dalliance. Not that I didn't take a look at them supping and chatting once or twice — from the rim to see the tepid dirty water the literati swam in . . . their heads bobbing, tilted, feigning interest. A lot of that — *interest*. Piss-poor on the passion side. And I said imagine yourself, Mattie, shining up to that fellow with the dainty feet and hands or that lady with a flea twitch in artistic green. Talk and interest. A stagnant pool. Think of yourself beholden to that dike with teeth like animal corn who runs the poetry review, or making sport of the whole scene while living it, as many did — the fucking literati. Imagine yourself, Mattie, so diluted. *I saw the world, and yet I was not seen* — once or twice from the rim before they knew my name.

"Born Matilda Le Doux on the day my mother died. Cursed with the love of poetry from an early age. Beaten with a strap for reading Tennyson. Whacked with the back of my father's hand for Longfellow and Poe. Hunger — Shelley. Darkness — Keats. I remember poets by my punishment. Neglecting the wash, the ironing, slops to the pigs, I read on. Kept it pure. Then lay in the barn with whoever at twelve, thirteen — as natural as the sheep and cows. Coarse. Raw. Farm boys and salesmen. Grand times. And I killed my father with it — oh, not rutting with the minister's son in the shadow of Indian Rock. Paid the old man back not with my disgrace but with reading while he died."

"I cannot —" Elizabeth said.

"*I can no more,*" said Mattie. "*Antony and Cleopatra,* he's in the act of dying. *Now my spirit is going; I can no more.* And dying my father had to watch me read the poems of William Butler Yeats, in his last agony watch me slowly turn the pages of *Responsibilities.* Feed that child a rusk. Tell your mother you found Mattie out. *Or, be secret and exult, because of all things known that is most difficult.* Jane never wrote a line, pathetic priss. Crochet, geraniums — all she was up to — a simple pudding now and then. Borderline case: the cranium small. Days of solitaire and television when it came. Afraid of stairs and shadows. It was our pact: I keep my sister and acquire her name. All minor stuff, my early work. Sonnets finely wrought. Careful imitations. Prizes, a bit of notoriety never claimed. Meanwhile I was Mattie, barmaid, typist, candy and cosmetic counter in the five-and-dime. Hosiery door to door. The factories. I had a Scandinavian foreman in Ansonia with the blondest testicles, fairest balls I've ever seen. A beauty shop on the Federal Road. I had a salesman for nets and curlers with a ready tongue —"

"I'm not afraid," Elizabeth said reasonably. The baby sucking from breast to breast was stupefied and smelled. Elizabeth could smell her own sour sweat and fear. She looked beyond the heavy black fry pan Big Mattie wafted as easily as a palm-leaf fan, looked out to the day. The day was ragged after the storm, but quieted, reformed. Stepping forward she said again, "I'm not afraid," heard the tremor in her voice.

"*I, a stranger and afraid in a world I never made.* Housman. Strong style but disappointment is not one of the grand themes. Sit down. Don't touch those pages. Tell your mother that Jane Le Doux was a rotten nom de plume, constricting and genteel. The shoddy craft of camouflage. I see that whole career as practice for the work to come — Mattie's poem. My flesh, my life, my world. I have gathered it all. I have looked upon my spectacle, not out of windows glassed and framed with a single view." Mattie puffed up and up as she spoke, the big body rocking gently, tipsy, inflated with her own words. "My time, my art, without vanity, without audience I have gathered it all. Tell your idle mother, though she will never understand what a trial it's been to have visitors when there's no time. *My thread is cut, and yet it is not spun.* I am only now approaching the first heart attack of Dwight David Eisenhower when I ran the liquor store on One-Nineteen, an era of false peace and plenty."

The fry pan fell before Big Mattie Le Doux slid exhausted to the kitchen floor. The young woman shoved her aside like a bale. But from the deadweight in the costume of a clown came words: "Tell your nosy mother I had it all, perfection of the life and of the work."

Elizabeth and her boy were weeping in the rocky field when the State Police came. The first man out of the car was Gus Muranis. The cops respectfully held back. "You're safe," Gus said repeatedly, touching his wife and child to make sure they were whole.

"We're safe," Elizabeth said and began a choking spasmodic laugh. Senselessly the baby laughed with her, then the cops.

Gus looked across at their car. "My poor darling," he said, "the damage is covered by comprehensive fire and theft."

Pulling herself up to the window Mattie saw them, the young family reunited, a conventional ending. Good-looking fellow, her type, dark complexion, broad shoulders. Clutching at his wife. "*I preferred,*" Mattie Le Doux spoke as always to herself, "*the irresponsible beauty of a stranger,*" and could not for her life recall whose line it was until a day later in the hospital it came to her, just as she passed to the Elysian fields.

At this hour the horizon disappeared. For an hour or so the bright sky and placid Caribbean Sea were one in a flat blue, like a primitive painting where depth has not been recorded. The hotel's yellow awnings and foreshortened avenue of princess palms were pasted against a naive streak of beach. Gilbert Lasser felt obliged to take advantage of his balcony after lunch. In a straw hat from one of the galleria shops and prescription sunglasses, he gave himself ten minutes of dangerous tropical sun and a long look at the expensive, uninhabited view. Paradise, pinned down by two preposterous thatched huts — one dispensing pale fruity drinks laced with rum, the other a constant chaffing of maracas in time with the electronic beat of native music. In the blank hours after lunch all such festive enterprises were suspended, as was the famous island breeze. Bert Lasser had the sense of a world shut off at the main and that whatever little energy remained flowed out of his own arms and legs as he stretched on the canvas lounge. The last human being observing his last coherent thought dwindle to mere consciousness, a loss of mortal power under the motionless sun.

As he expected, life was unreal at Palmas del Mar. Two days was enough, yet his plane reservation would keep him here until the following night. Now that the conference, or his part in it, was over, it was dismal, lingering on alone for the fresh pineapple and dips in the mammoth swimming pool. The idea of mixing with the businessmen whom he had lectured was equally dispiriting. Not that they weren't good sorts, enjoying themselves. And they had asked most incisive questions about the problems of individual commitment to the corporate undertaking, the distinctions between subjective and objective reasoning. It wasn't that he would patronize these energetic men who asked him to come out on the spectacular golf course or for a day of deep-sea fishing. On the contrary, they would indulge him, talk up to him a bit continuing the "question period," or down — treat him to smutty stories all of which he'd heard at a recent meeting of neurosurgeons. They would drink less, laugh less with the little professor. Bert Lasser knew he was a formal man: the trim beard and mustache, the assertive stride, the careful tailoring were neither military nor professorial. He had not taught in years.

It went back, this air of assurance, this gentlemanly bearing that seemed a reference to another time, back to the days when Gilbert with his sissy name had to walk the block of roughnecks with his schoolbooks, wearing talmudic dark suits. Coming down from the flat over the market he was abused physically and verbally by the neighborhood children whose parents bought their daily bread and milk from the Lassers on account. Taunted and tripped, the pages of his notebook scattered in the sewer, he had learned that it was best never to cower or dodge, but to walk calmly like Samson among the Philistines, like Ronald Colman in *The Light That Failed* facing the Indian hordes. "Bertie" . . . "Rabbi Ben-Gilbert" . . . "the mad scientist." His contour map of the Caucasian Mountains (flour-paste lumped majestically between the Black and Caspian Seas) was crushed, peed on by an old yellow dog. His molecular model of hydrochloric acid was dissolved into toothpicks and broken drinking straws that Mickey Sconzo twirled out of his ears. Skinny, secretive, bright — as a kid Bert Lasser knew why he was mocked. He had what all those poor kids wanted in the thirties — carfare, a way out. When he was thirteen he copied a motto from Santayana onto a shirt cardboard — "The acme of life is to understand life" — and tacked it up in his room, where he had everything he needed: a slide rule, microscope, *Roget's Thesaurus*. And marched on like a wise little soldier to his classroom success.

It was a curse to him, this continual understanding, as well as a comfort, like a physical disability that gave him certain privileges but held him back from the real game. He was never angry enough, brutal enough, never obsessed. When he understood that he would always do good science, not great science, he moved into the gray area of consultation and foundation work — areas of larger understanding. When his first marriage failed it was with his complete understanding that two disparate natures happy enough as working pals in the laboratory might become cool colleagues in the bedroom. Bert Lasser understood his hatred of poverty, fascism, unjust war, the decline and fragmentation of values: the list was admirable. He understood that the cozy delights of his second marriage replaced dreams of fame and passion that he'd never sought.

Understandably, he disliked his room at Palmas del Mar, which he now entered from the balcony, while finding it quite good of its kind — the furniture was rattan, the carpet pleasantly swirled with palms, more than tasteful, the temperature in his control. A slight tint to the sliding glass doors corrected the glare of Caribbean sun. He had not wanted to come to a resort, but the money was good and Bert understood that he liked the adulation of men who made twice, three times his salary. He liked the idea of himself as the fastidious gnome reminding powerful men that there were questions they had not asked in years, premises they never challenged when they bought and sold a national resource, small countries, the life of a city. Assumptions that he could flick over with a clever argument, the brightest schoolboy still. This time he had wanted Maude to come: she had her patients; she had an insignificant growth like a tiny bubble poised on her eyelid. A minor chalazion.

"Isn't that a beautiful name," she'd said. "It sounds like a constellation." But it was annoying as a mite and she was to have it off in the doctor's office.

So Bert had come to Puerto Rico alone like a trouper. And his act had gone well. He had spoken after the first luncheon to a relatively sober crowd (they were pharmaceutical executives and research men) on the possibility of moral consensus as a basis for responsible decision. His talk followed by a conservationist who showed lurid slides of chemical waste. Calling Maude twice that night, missing her running commentary on the rich tourists, ersatz food. He called her now to confess his boredom and thought when he heard her taped voice on the private line that this must be her day at the eye doctor. In a reasonable moment he packed his bag, his papers, and put on the light worsted suit for traveling, wrote a note to a young man he was to drink with at five, and went down to the lobby.

The young man was problematic, had dogged him down at breakfast and already blurred with rum collins had pursued him to the pool at ten, then to lunch. Sober and drunk he told Bert that he had studied moral philosophy at Harvard with Rawls and that he still read whatever it was he read that proved he was respectable though he made eighty thousand dollars a year. A romantic young biochemist who'd sold out a bit early, the boy had a hungry alcoholic look. Bert Lasser said that he was a company man himself who doled out money made by a corporation larger than most pill factories: he spoke to doctors, lawyers, merchants — a traveling salesman with wares that were quaint and out of style.

So the successful, self-destructive fellow got an evasive note phrased like a maxim in a fortune cookie: "Pursue the useful. More often than not it is good"; and Bert, feeling irresponsible, took a cab forty miles into San Juan. Ten days before Christmas the only possibility of a flight to New York was a cancellation in first class, a nighttime flight. He wandered, taking a bus to the university, a cab to the Governor's Mansion, then walked with some purpose in the old city of San Juan.

He knew this place. The narrow streets of prosperous shops and clean restaurants were charming but real. Yard goods, shoes, records and tapes. Even the tourist pottery and baskets were acceptable here as part of the island industry. He knew this part of town, had come here with his first wife on a delayed honeymoon after she finished her dissertation. It was much the same in the fifties, this old city, crowded and noisy, perhaps less American without the feedback from the barrios in New York. Then the poverty was visible down alleys, in courtyards. Now the bums, if they were bums, looked fine in the public squares. The trash cans were improved. The political slogans calling for the independence of Puerto Rico were more sophisticated scrawls these days and a bilingual pamphlet thrust into his hand as he walked up to the fortifications was written in standard jargon of the left.

He knew this view, had stood here with Sara Ann Phipps, held hands, kissed. As the photos were taken to memorialize their romance, the romance was fading. Out of their lab in Cambridge they were not a necessary team. Decent young people, they had strained for more than an interest in each other. He remembered that she was boyish, that she looked awkward on the tropical evenings dressed to charm. They had walked up here arm in arm, looking out over the Atlantic, where sailors had come for gold and youth, knowing (as they would) the long history of the place, not guessing that their own history would be brief. They had stayed together long enough for Sara to complete her next project — having a child.

The sea was deeply shadowed but untroubled, the waves flapping gently at the rocks below. Bert had seen this end of day with Sara Ann. At the same time of year, for she had finished her work on schedule. Earnest and scholarly, they had timed their trip for the Christmas break and come here on a careful budget. He knew that the late sun would wash its reddish light over the adobe of the fort and the old church. He must ask Maude, who saw beneath the surface of things so quickly, why he had returned here. Why had he not thought for a moment of the ill-fated honeymoon when he accepted the invitation to Palmas del Mar. Thirty years ago he had entered the church in San José reluctantly, a Jew, a scientist, never having wandered far from Boston or New York. His wife, of puritan stock, would not cover her head in the Catholic church. This was architecture to them — the rare gothic vaulting, the later bronze and filigree adornments — not a house of God. He would ask Maude why he came, why he was so eager to enter the dark vestibule this time and sit in the quiet without guidebook or camera. There were no tourists. It was the hour for pineapple and rum.

A woman came toward him from a side altar where she had lit a candle to the Virgin. A beautiful woman of forty perhaps, dressed in a pale linen suit, immaculate and cool. She was a Puerto Rican woman who knew how to move and dress in her climate. It seemed to Bert Lasser that she was coming to him. Her eyes steady with dull sorrow were fixed on him, drawing him to her, but she hesitated and went into the pew directly in front of his as though in the empty church she sought the comfort of his presence or an audience. But she withdrew at once into an absorbing round of prayers. In this solitude she crossed herself with a hand that was graceful, well manicured. She wore diamonds in moderation and smelled of a fine light scent, not perfume that announced a price. He felt powerless, as he had on the balcony of Palmas del Mar, simply watching as she languidly repeated the sign of the cross at intervals in her mysterious and private rite. The hair on her head was lustrous and dark, not dead black. A glint of red streaked the close curls cropped to a triangular bush at her nape. Weighted and dreamlike, her breathing extended to him, monitored his own quick pulse to a slow beat of desire. He watched the programmed flick of her sad eyes and the motion of her lips like a fervent kiss that brought an end to some plea. What was she asking — that a man be faithful, a parent die without pain, a child not break her heart? Why was she asking that her personal tragedy be accepted as part of a largely discredited enterprise? Wasn't her life enough with that exceptional beauty? Who in God's name was she asking? But her belief as she knelt in San José was assured and impenetrable. The woman did not notice the bearded gentleman again until he rose and walked out after her into the bright pinkish light.

"May I —" Bert Lasser said, taking her arm, but he had no idea what it was that he suggested.

"I'm just there," she said without a trace of accent, waving her car keys, dismissing him kindly. He looked carefully at her body. With her arm raised, the linen jacket opened and there was a show of white lace under a low-cut blouse, an outline of breast, even the rim of hard nipple through silk for him to observe. Her skirt was deeply creased exactly at the crotch from the prolonged time kneeling at her prayers. The woman was perhaps older than he had guessed, certainly taller now that she stood facing him. Her lovely head somewhat elongated. Straight line from the conquistadores. She put her hand out to him as though he were to kiss it or address it with a bow.

"Señora," Bert Lasser said, fumbling with her fingertips.

She repaid him with the intimate smile of someone who has told her story. "Thanks," she said for whatever he'd given — his attention, sexual reassurance — and she walked off to a little car with the sticker of the Audubon Society on its windshield. San Juan plates.

Maude would intuit rightly that the doomed young man from Harvard in combination with the self-dramatizing woman at prayer had made him think of Teddy. The Reverend Theodore Lasser was assistant pastor of Saint Clement's, an Episcopalian parish. Florida: Palm Beach. He was Gilbert Lasser's son. His stepmother, Maude (who had eaten an awkward dinner with him once), might push it and say that Bert took the trip to Puerto Rico because Teddy was nearby in the sun. Wasn't it natural? A yearly Christmas present, a few letters, fewer visits — the enlightened way in which the boy's life had been arranged after Bert's divorce and Sara Phipps's appropriate remarriage had not allowed for deeper feelings, the irrational connection of flesh and blood. Maude, who construed the simple matters, schooled in facing the emotional facts, would tell him how perfectly understandable it was for a man to go looking for his son.

It was unreasonable to Bert: he moved like a counter in a board game, thrust forward by the spin of a wobbly arrow or the draw of a card. Leave luxury hotel. Reserve flight. Tour city. Cancel New York. Fly to Miami. Sleep in pasteboard motel. Wake to drive the coast north. Drive past the miles of glittering condominiums where everything is new, clean, nothing oppressively personal. The very shimmer of tropical foliage and imported sod stuck flat around the buildings is unremarkable, as in an ordinary child's version of eternal summer. Drive the miles: easy times, life's rewards. Dream as you drive the rented car, which is bloated and tinny, nothing you would own, that you will find the son you gave up so reasonably. You will find him a man ministering to Cuban refugees, counseling troubled families. Find him comforting the old who have come to die in a warm climate. You will forgive him the years of mumbo jumbo in the seminary (surely some of it directed at you), and the barbaric ritual of his ordination, which you would not attend. Forgive your son his belief, which is no more in this age than a commitment to social work and mild psychotherapy. Forgive his calling as you once forgave or took into account his adoration of older boys who trashed a dean's office, burned draft cards, fled the civil guard like desperate men. Drive sixty miles of El Dorado and admit to your lost romantic kid he may be right: it is more important to change the world than to understand it.

Saint Clement's when Bert found it was indistinguishable from the surrounding mansions, many of them with bell towers and heavy convent gates, all of them executed in the smooth white stucco of Spanish revival that aped humble adobe. These glamorous haciendas were the size of municipal buildings, their grounds like public gardens. At nine in the morning there was no one to be seen enjoying the grandeur. Saint Clement's appeared a poor relation on its massive corner plot, suffering a subcutaneous crumble of the face. Front and center, a dry fountain of Moorish design, a Coke can fading in its basin, cracked blue and yellow tiles dull under a layer of silt. But the grass of Saint Clement's was kept intensely green; the cypress, camellias and bird of paradise as perfectly Floridian as any in the neighborhood.

And here there was life: a dune buggy and a brace of white Mercedes sat in the circular drive. Here was a blackboard announcing Evensong, Communion and the associate rector's name, Rev. Theodore Lasser. A promotion, Bert thought, with fatherly pride. My son the priest, but the tired Jewish joke seemed more than ever crude.

Inside it was cool and dark, plainer than the church in old San Juan that had been mucked about through the centuries. Saint Clement's was pure 1920s, subtle as money could make the Spanish rip-off and charmingly askew as to cultural intent. Why Episcopalians should want to imitate this patently Catholic heritage, Bert Lasser could never comprehend. True, there were no statues, no votive lights or gilt. The church was secular in its good taste.

Voices in the distance . . . somewhere behind the plain wood altar, voices and laughter. As he approached, his feet rang out on the polished tiles. No one heard. He thought of calling out — *Teddy?* If that name was in use. *Teddy?* As he had called blindly in railway stations, at bus depots, hoping he would recognize his visiting son. Whether matted and unclean like a stray dog or clipped and newly varnished for the theological seminary, Ted Lasser had always had the grace to identify himself to his embarrassed father.

Bert's footsteps were intrusive. He could hear his city stride to be crass, inappropriate, and he slowed down, became conscious of stealing quietly toward the voices. This cool church was in the care of his son. Ever so gently he sidled along a white wall to a small room hung with starched white vestments. Thick candles on a shelf. The musty smell of incense. A rack of embroidered garments, gold, red and purple. Velvet. Silks. Jesus — all too Spanish — stretched in a transcendent bloodstained agony upon the cross. Bert thought, looking at the gouged red wounds, forgive that personal undertaking. There's progress to be made on fake premises. Try to believe that when you meet your son. The voices came over the airy transom of carved wooden fretwork. He had the cinematic notion of a dusky señorita who might peer through, give him the signal of a rose or fan — but the door itself was massive, blackened to look like ancient oak secured with iron hasps (an evil reference to the Inquisition) and at eye level, as though made for Gilbert Lasser to eavesdrop, there was the narrowest slit.

"Dear ladies," the Reverend Theodore Lasser said, "I can never thank you adequately. One hundred and twenty-eight dollars and thirty-three cents. Not a splendid

return on our effort. [Laughter.] And certainly beneath your dignity, Polly [more laughter], but our
Christmas jumble was a necessity. They seem to want
white-elephant touches that remind them of the old
hometown, these awful bake sales and potluck suppers,
which, in fact, I doubt they ever attended in their ricky-
ticky postwar developments." He was a sleek young man,
small-boned, deeply tanned, his fair hair streaked by the
sun — looking absolutely a wonder this morning in a
white linen suit and sandals. The black shirtfront and roman collar seemed the whimsy of a fashion photogra-
pher, as did the high-backed chair in which he sat, tooled
leather suitable for a Velázquez prince of the church. The
room, the Reverend Mr. Lasser's "study," was furnished
with Persian rugs, English pottery and an organized wall
of stereo equipment that gleamed from white Formica
shelves. As though to underscore the split, the priest had
hung a poster of Constable cows blown up out of proportion next to dizzy graphics plugging the Modern Jazz
Quartet.

"The Lord giveth and the Lord taketh away," Theodore Lasser said in a nasal voice that slipped about with
British inflections. "Saint Clement's enjoyed half a century of serenity before the condominia were built. They
are the cross to bear." [Girlish laughter from his audience
of three.]

Three matrons so anonymously and expensively
dressed, so well preserved there was no guessing at their
ages and, Bert Lasser thought, almost no point in guessing at their sex. Polly — who distinguished herself by

having more angles to her body, a careless authority, an incomparable sportiness — stood over a refectory table strewn with domestic litter: cups without saucers, toasters, cocktail glasses, trivets, Parcheesi and ringtoss, a tangled heap of costume jewelry.

"What in God's name?" she asked.

"In God's name exactly," said the Reverend Mr. Lasser scaling his irony down to light sincerity. "In His name we put that junk in boxes. They will want a flea market at Mardi Gras, more jumble. They will want Lent as they never observed it, vespers and Palm Sunday. They are hungry for rituals to fill the day and for religious trappings to ease them into night." [Solemnity from the little audience.] The three women of Palm Beach were enchanted, as they were each Sunday morning: his voice — eastern, northern, Harvard as once they knew or at least dreamed it. Theodore Lasser's resignation and world-weary pauses were eloquent. The determined goodness of his aphoristic speech reminded them of the likable heroes in novels they swapped, respected novels written by gentlemen surprisingly Christian, surprising Episcopalian. Only Polly — smarter, richer, with a bishop in her background — might guess as she packed trash into a Wild Turkey carton that her confessor's delivery had been picked up from the Anglican clique at the seminary. And she thanked God that sort of thing went on at all.

"There will be civil strife within the altar society," Ted Lasser said. "The old guard will want the usual holly and ivy, the single spray of red camellias for the midnight mass, Christmas as you have known it at Saint Clement's, restrained and thoughtful. Now we must open our hearts to the painfully obvious. The new people will expect an excess of potted poinsettia with floral bows and funereal mums. A Mrs. Hazel Pepper has donated an illuminated crèche with blinking star for the lawn. There are three hundred 'living units' — dare we call them homes? — within this parish that for all their advertised luxe are raw as aboriginal huts. It has happened here. Now we must accept Saint Clement's as a missionary post. By His grace we have been awarded this task and with His love we shall fulfill it. These men and women displaced from days of gain, restless in their pursuit of pleasure, uncomfortable with peace, have come to us. We look upon a ghetto in our own backyard. Buena Vista, Palm Terrace, Gloriette Manor. These are the costly slums of today. As Christians we welcome these people to our reading club, to our chapter of Alcoholics Anonymous — yes, even to our choir, where they will raise their voices with us in a little less Saint Clement's oratorio, a little more schlock *de Noël.*" [Laughter.]

The Reverend Mr. Lasser rose from his chair and with his own fine hands placed a useless alarm clock in the store of debris for future sale. Lamentable, he said, and taking up a little leather book, a worn prayer book or breviary, he toyed with its satin marker, a signal that he would now withdraw to another world. Separately and coyly they worshiped him, three girls grown old. Theodore Lasser was all they wanted in a man. Under his banner they would meet the alien tribe — the retired shopkeepers, postal clerks, firemen who had come to live on the reclaimed swampland so near their church. Give way, extend themselves, all so lamentable. Edified by their own virtue and resolve, they left to shop for the last Christmas presents, further cheer.

Behind the heavy timbered door Gilbert Lasser turned sharply from the slit through which he had spied on his son's shrewd performance. He walked at a soldierly clip past the high-church costumes, through the unctuous odor and sanctimonious half-light, out to the remorseless sun, where Polly and those others dawdled by their fancy cars. Still in the glow, he presumed, of the Reverend Mr. Lasser's self-serving lecture on the sin of Pride. He did not have the heart to look upon whatever idolatry Teddy practiced, left to his priestly room alone.

Drive to the Miami airport, where a tape of Bing Crosby rings out "Adeste Fideles," against the announcement of departing flights. Pay for the car. At any expense get the next flight home. Tell yourself, Bert Lasser said, that it is unreasonable to suffer this — anguish or furious heartbreak in a game of chance.

When Gus bought the car he was giddy. More than lighthearted, he could feel the flutter in his chest, happiness rising in him, so he spoke hastily to a clerk to tie down his words, then signed his check with a flourish. *Constantine Muranis* — the grand and indecipherable signature of a successful man. Ingeniously he then had the car shipped to Muranis Superette.

His day in court: That morning he had won another delay in the Amptrex case. He had submitted in separately argued motions that the material of a personal nature to be found in both the Atlanta and Louisville files could not be investigated. He wanted not victory to his credit but the brilliant stall. His motion, written under the surveillance of a senior partner, would buy Amptrex another six or eight months, during which time the administration would change. Republicans in, it would take another year before the new regime began to untangle the transcripts of evidentiary hearings, millions of documents, at last count one hundred and fourteen briefs. Just the words constituting Amptrex were awesome. And what to Gus was the beauty in this case — fragmentation. It would never come to trial. He had a triumphant steak at Christ Cella with members of his firm, watching a senator drink his lunch with a group of abstemious Japanese businessmen. A Christmas wreath hung over the bar and that is when he decided to take the afternoon, walk up Fifth Avenue and buy something memorable to give to Elizabeth.

The car in the window caught his attention at once. A dark green with lustrous depths as though lacquered. The heavy chrome of the wheels and bumpers entirely satisfying. Sneaky headlights. The body low, extravagant. How many days in one life do you pull off a major coup against the Department of Justice? How often do you get a postponement that allows you to float up from Foley Square to a thirty-dollar sirloin? It was cold, drizzling — he had not noticed in his euphoria — a rotten winter day with only determined shoppers. He should take some time now — that's what people did in winter, went to islands, the Yucatán. Take the baby, all of them go to lie in the sun.

In the famous toy store he did not ask the price. "I'll take the car," Gus said in a great hurry. "Yes, the car on display. It's for sale?" Then he had thought to send it to his parents' address so that on Christmas it would be a surprise for Elizabeth as well as his boy.

And there the car was in Astoria, Queens, a miniature MG convertible in the small living room above the Superette. A real radio set into the wooden dashboard, authentic seat belts, stick shift and a sensational canvas top, which he raised now to the delight of his mother. The car sat between the sofa and the television set where the coffee table made of tiles from Salonika should be. It displaced the chalky bust of Homer and the album with the Muranis grandchildren smiling for the Instamatic. It displaced photographs of his sisters on their wedding days, even Gus in his cap and gown. Anyway the girls lived on in the neighborhood and were in and out of the store with their kids. Not Gus. He lived in Westchester, another world.

Maria Muranis had invited all her friends up to view the car, a visible sign of her son's achievement. A diminutive woman in a crisp housedress, she sat on the edge of a footstool the better to look up to her enormous son. She had fed him roast beef from the store, her own pastry, thick Greek coffee. Now she feasted her eyes upon him as he tapped the rubber tire and unscrewed the gas tank cap. The baby, Jason Muranis, could crawl now and he was strong. He could pull himself up by that chrome bumper to a standing position.

"He's not going to hurt himself?" Maria Muranis asked.

"It's a toy."

"Some toy." She laughed and dabbed at her eyes. When Gus came she was given to easy weeping. This big man with the money, the beautiful wife and baby. This big man in the beautiful suits, that he should stop on his way to the airport when he had work with the government in Washington, D.C., or stop on his way back to Rye, to his wife and baby, moved her to tears. Her son had a gorgeous house on acreage. On the twenty-fourth they would take the toy car in the delivery truck up there to surprise . . . She would make butter cookies, though Maria would not bring presents until later, the Greek Christmas, because Gus said keep the old ways and what he said was in her mind the law.

Maude goes to the doctor's walking all the way. She has allowed herself time to walk a good distance in order to take her mind off the operation that will be performed at eleven o'clock upon her eye. It is minor surgery, a tiny cyst on the lower eyelid has become an annoyance and must be removed. She thinks of herself, somewhat vainly, as a tough old dame. There is an air of risk about the day as it begins: the unique nature of her appointment; the word *surgery* casts its drama upon her ordinary movements. Turning the key in her lock, ringing for the elevator, she favors herself, her story, and is delighted when she comes up with the phrase "under the knife." Maude goes to the doctor, walking the miles with energy, seeing more than the usual sights. When the cyst is removed she feels no pain but returns in a cab like an invalid, or like a willing soldier who never saw battle and comes home in personal defeat.

I walked all the way. It was Friday, somewhat gloomy as I turned my back on the dark bramble of Riverside Park and headed to Broadway. The season had come. On that gray morning Christmas lights twitched on and off neurotically in an Indian boutique, the first of many. All my shops — cleaners, fish market, shoe repair — were hand-decorated, the efforts of men and women I knew at least by sight, as familiar to me as ghost figures on Main Street in my hometown. I stopped at the newsstand wanting something. The *Times* had been delivered and read at the crack of dawn. I wanted something to amuse myself. My doctor, a young woman who is *molto* serious, puts out U.S. *News and World Report, The Economist* in her office. I wanted something light: Gilbert was away.

My patients were canceled. I was about to have an operation, after all. The fashion magazines were too foolish, pages of clownish costumes all costing hundreds if not thousands of dollars. The models looked burned out this year or drugged, with heavy lids and slack mouths about to dribble on their sequins and lace. I took up *House and Garden* with a primitive thrill. What I wanted — a blue spruce beside a massive fireplace, a cradle jammed with pinecones, old teddy bears. Popcorn balls in an Edwardian compote. What I needed — a recipe for eggnog mousse, a text useless as a poem. And I thought, as the man dealt me change, never again will I find time or care to stuff a goose and lay it out with parsnip boats, or steam an apple pudding. Married to a Jew, a man of science, I put a few greens on the mantel at Christmas, wear a red dress that is short and out of style. We go to visit my daughter in Westchester with modest gifts. So it's all fantasy about Christmas, a holiday that makes my youthful patients manic or depressed. It's why I went to Dr. Blau that Friday: they will need me at Christmas and at New Year's, which for many of them remains a bleak beginning.

The season had come. Trees and wreaths being sold all along upper Broadway. Once again I noticed that the traffic changes, naturally thickens, as I approach Columbus Circle and that I always feel so keenly that I have left my neighborhood and gone downtown. This is the city, with city noises, cabs screeching, buses grunting, heaving, sighing in packs. The imperial back entrance to Central Park with its European statuary, like awful trophies saluting civic barns across the way and the cold glamour of the GM Tower. People moving on purpose. The subway. Connections. And I saw dancers, most certainly dancers, two men and a girl with long backs, heads balanced effortlessly high, their big sacks with ballet slippers and leotards slung on their shoulders, heading to Lincoln Center.

I thought of Ana, how she had flexed her arms when she came in the door and always met me with a turn, half a bourrée. It would be the right time for her to be with these dancers going to warm up. Early on she had been a snowflake during this season, or warrior mouse. Professional, never bored with the routine, Ana had become the Sugarplum Fairy. That was over and done. She said she did not miss dancing. Married to the doctor, she taught Spanish children to brush their teeth and bathe, to eat vegetables, drink milk. As a young married couple they bought expensive modern furniture, went to new movies, dined out. Ana had ripped a tendon in her thigh, so it was over and done, her body making the choice that had so troubled her mind. I had gone to their apartment on the East Side to admire a raw-silk couch and she seemed perfectly happy, rested for the first time in her young life. The case closed and I suppose I count it a success.

I walked to Central Park South, which I hate, the stretch to the Plaza with chilly hotels. Hookers stepping into limousines, indistinguishable from guests — I didn't know that morning as I went to surgery, I will never know, what's the attraction of this dead commercial splendor. Who are these people with all that matched luggage and a fistful of tips? Men in Stetsons. Women disappearing into furs. Arabian princes. Not real people. And I recall my pleasing contempt at their impoverishment: this facade all they knew of the city, this strip of prime real estate, which I have always thought inauthentic, second-rate. A fine cold drizzle kept me at attention as I walked the last blocks into the Christmas rush feeling it was good for me, even the ring of hysterical disorder spreading out from Bloomingdale's. I am so much closed in. Closed in my office with patients, their never-ending fables of self-concern, that I seldom see the light of day. It was good to be out.

What I had not expected was the needle coming at my eye, then the knife. But how was she to anesthetize it, cut the lid?

"Steady," she said.

"God help me."

And strictly: "You must not move."

"God help me, no." I lay steady with fear, the sharp knife at my eye. Like a Swiss tool my mother had for carving wood. I did not move as the surgeon came at me and asked if we had seen a popular Broadway show. Her little distraction like a sleight of hand. "My husband doesn't like musicals," I said in all innocence. As my mouth flooded with the waters of nausea, she stepped back. The deed was done. Dr. Blau's hands when she pulled them out of the surgical gloves were perfectly smooth, unused, the nails enameled rose as mine had been once — when I did nothing at all. What I had not counted on was the bandage, a large affair strapped from forehead to chin.

"Oh, no —"

"How do you propose to keep the wound clean?" she scolded. "It is just for a day." There was no pain but she warned that I was prone to these small growths. As I could see, they were ephemeral, nothing at all.

A good deal to me. Feeling for my purse, my coat, catching the office-art and jolly orange curtains with one eye, swinging my whole body round to get the set of the door. I never thought I would be trembling, clutching at the walls, unsure of every distance — or that in the elevator people would draw back from me in horror, patients most of them in this medical building, with real ailments and disease. It's nothing at all: I wanted to soothe them with a lie. One might call it cosmetic, the removal of a mote. I am over fifty and I'm not in pain. But they continued to hold themselves apart and at the ground floor stood back for me, that I might make my way with drunk precision past the Christmas tree, which was bushy Scotch pine in plastic under a dusting of eternal snow. Boxes wrapped as presents lay scattered at the base. Unsteady, past the reception desk, walnut Formica, closed-circuit TV, red phones (I felt I must get all details with one eye), to the smudged glass door, which two men rushed to open for me. Thank You. Thank You. I'm just over fifty, not suffering. But there's a limit to what comes to mind and what you say.

The cabdriver told me without preliminaries that his son was deaf. Wonderful thing — how the kid lives with disability, how he does numbers and computer skills like he can hear. It's the people around apparently don't know how to live with disability.

I said nothing, but listed to the side with my good eye to see the dark noon, pavements now slick with rain, all the hearty two-eyed people heading for shops and restaurants. Central Park was exhausting — the assault of open space, the articulate network of shiny branches against the dull sky. I could now feel my eyelash flutter and catch against the gauze without pain. At my door the cabby shouted as he must to his deaf son. "I'm not going to help you." I lurched to the sidewalk. "Do for yourself. That's the way."

I never counted on panic in the lobby — the doorman's shock, queasy neighbors and delivery men. A mother shielded her child from the sight of me. Why were they loitering here at midday, all of them. All of them gaping, excited, as though they were at the scene of a particularly fine accident. Mrs. Lasser, my God! I think it was in response to their cries I gave them their drama and let a flock of them escort me to the elevator as I fumbled for my key with a pitiful smile. Mrs. Lasser?

"It is a chalazion," I said, leaving them awed.

Safe inside, I saw myself for the first time in the amber light, kept dim for my patients. In the front-hall mirror filmed with age, my poor face withered and ashy supported a vast display of white bandage. On a dry and colorless lower plain, my mouth was etched in by the cruel incision of years. My one gallant eye was red with its efforts. Disfigured, I made a guttural noise as though I were in pain. Turning, I saw the mail under the door. Then pivoted in the direction of the kitchen, where the refrigerator began its weary groan. I was astonished that ordinary life should wander on while I bore my injury alone.

Gilbert Lasser, cold, fastidious man: my husband was off on some mission — to say that the earth was no longer round or that our morality is best founded in self-interest. His windy considerations of the world-at-large. He had abandoned me to this place, this apartment with its mis-

erable houseplants and worn chairs. Out back, I had half-
view of a diverting air shaft. At front, the treat of rapes
and murder, dog business in the narrow strip of park.
This was to be my end. No porch. No trees. No grass.
No comfort in the local legend of a rock. Garbage scows
on the discredited Hudson. Cool, deliberate man:
"Maude," he had said of my chalazion, "it will be less
than a toothache, more than a benign mole." He cannot
feel, but always speaks at me in persistent editorials. Off
basking in the Caribbean sun. Freeloading in Paradise. I
would not lower myself to call and say it's painful here.
Alone in a rented place, over fifty years old . . . under
the knife.

With no further provocation, I started on Elizabeth as
I tottered to the bedroom with the mail and my magazine. Ungrateful girl. I had made a world for her. The
costly years of training: her scales and noisy exercises —
maddening while I worked over my courses for Columbia, preparing myself for life. It was not painless, discov-
ering all the years I had been passive, duped. The muck
that rose to the surface, warped and disfigured, when I
first came to this city. Cruel, incriminating fragments of
the past. At my expense. While the great waste went on
around me — her Steinway, Italian lessons, diction, fenc-
ing, dance. I remembered the outrageous price of her
georgette recital gown. In this version I had sold my house
for her. Left a warmhearted circle of friends. On Seventy-
sixth Street I had waited up for my daughter at night,
long after the heat went off, long after the streets were
safe, patiently reading on — the cases of advanced

narcissism, hysteria and sexual dysfunction — until her key turned in the latch. Supper for her on the stove at midnight. Oh, I was glad to be of any use.

She had paid me with silence. Sold out in Westchester. Gagged in her house with a lawn and trees, a baby. With her money and her husband, the corporation stud. Ungrateful child. She will have a proper Christmas wreath, I have no doubt, on a real front door.

I said: "This morning I was operated on. How is the baby? I'm here alone. It was nothing — surgery. The pain will begin now as the day wears on."

Next I had a go at the mail — bills, cards, an invitation to glogg that would launch the New Year. Greetings from my brother: KEVIN FAIN, PLASTIC AND RECONSTRUCTIVE SURGERY. Oh, that was grand — the impersonal office stationery to feed this smoldering self-pity. My good eye marched back and forth across the page. Kevin's words bled from line to line. Did I still have the German beersteins? He remembered them as echt bad taste. Send them for Charlene, who was heavily into kitsch. And did I have the nude Kewpie doll wearing a stethoscope and carrying a doctor's case? Their house was worth half a million. Semiretirement was contemplated in the Phoenix area or maybe Santa Fe. (Part-time tailor, would Kevin tuck one breast, clip half a nose?) Charlene was exhibiting Lucite in a beautiful space. Send the beer steins express.

The Bavarian stein (there was only one) I had given away, thank God, to a voice coach who recognized scenes from *Tannhäuser* in the posturing of those fair maids and knights. The Kewpie doll I doubt existed, except in Kevin's fantasies of his New England childhood, all of it dowdy, silly as an old radio show, heavy kitsch. Pressing on, I flung the whining notices from all the goodness folks across the room. Save. Defend. Aid. Feed.

What had I ever done but listen to youthful troubles at the going rate; suggest answers to obvious questions: Was that better? He upset you? Are you saying that it hurt? I had applied Band-Aids to large gaping wounds. It was bitter news to think that I had chosen my profession more to heal myself than others: treatment implies disease. Worse to think that I had understood life out of books, trusting that answers should be there. As a therapist I was totally inadequate. One-eyed voyeur. Finally there was nothing but the ceiling to stare at as I lay on my bed begging to be wiped out, made blank. But I saw that white paint on plaster as an unrelenting screen, projected there the early years of my marriage to Frank Dowd. I saw our first apartment near the Law School in New Haven. Our wrought-iron coffee table. Gummy textured prints of Utrillo and Cézanne. A glossy philodendron. Frank studying in our prize Danish-modern chair. With my eye closed I saw him still, look up at me with such desire as I held a steaming casserole above the dining ta-ble we had made ourselves from a lumberyard flush door. It was that time I saw when we were saving for a tele-vision set and conceded, after much glib argument, our loss of faith. And I remember that next I dropped the hot lid, broke a wedding present, and how bitterly I cried.

Opening my eye, there was Elizabeth. Mother, what have they done to you? Oh, Mother, what have they done? Something of that sort. I suppose in phoning her it's what I'd aimed at, this piteous scene. She fed me beef broth and crackers. Sponged off my hands and feet. Elizabeth had dumped the baby with her neighbor's maid and here was my girl fetching aspirin though there was not a moment's pain. Nursing me, she read from *House and Garden:* " 'The fluted pilaster was discovered under an existing layer of asphalt tile. Only the plinth and cornice . . .' " Dimming the light, smoothing the pillow's edge, Elizabeth read on: " 'Working from a neutral palette, Mr. Pear floated the entire room in biscuit and beige. . . .' Stop, Mother. Stop laughing! 'As Christmas approaches, Mrs. Barnstable puts out a rustic bin of scarlet pippins. . . .' Stop that laughing, you'll ruin your eye. 'Cream, brandy, vanilla bean unite in traditional splendor.' "

When I awoke . . . those standard dreams we told as children, horrors of the chase, terrifying precipice, evil figure in a killer's hat . . . "and then I woke up," we'd say, as if the dream were nonsense or untrue. But what I had dreamed actually — driving with an old lady. I am in the back seat and not troubled by her speeding, swooping the curves, shooting stop signs. Death is a funny business. She is smoking. It is not my mother, though she says he was never so good-looking as the boy. That boy is Kevin. We are in a shop with gaudy windows, trying on shoes that never fit. I am telling a story to a man. I am telling him passages from the Old Testament about clinical detachment, about *lymantria nervosa*, about repression. Heavily freckled, he does not . . . with a prominent nose, he does not, though it is immediate and urgent, know that I have dreamed that sentence: *Death is a funny business.* Then I woke with drifting sorrowful pleasure and the room was familiar around me. Bed in semidarkness under the habitual glow of city light. I had survived. Old wicker chairs turned to a river view. The wad of gauze and tape on my face was not surprising. Then I heard a note struck. A above high C. C-sharp. Next a trial run on the dusty keys, a chord struck, off-tune. Stumbling just once against the dresser, calculating the walls and doors like an expert with my disability, I made my way toward it, the music. I ran to the living-room arch. Elizabeth sat at the baby grand. She did not see or hear me, for the piano was pushed off facing the window, discarded behind the couch. She was looking at a score now, turning pages.

When she found her place Elizabeth sang. *Pie Jesu. Grant them rest. Grant them eternal rest.* Her voice was centered, agile and pure. It was the soprano melody from the Fauré *Requiem,* a piece she'd studied and sung in concert. Her first professional solo in New York. She stood now to get her breathing right and saw me, gave a nod of rec-ognition, but did not miss a note. My daughter sang in a gentle ecstasy. I'm the last one to say, but she reached celestial heights.

When it was done we smiled at each other foolishly, until she said, "Stop that, Mother. Stop crying." But I was not. Awkwardly, she grabbed for her coat and hat. Gruff, looking at the walls and floor, she said that she had started in the fall, after wrecking the car. Singing at home. At first there was a clot in her throat, a stoppage of phlegm or blood to dislodge. She had no voice at first, could not really sing a nursery rhyme or jingle, and one day, performing a menial task, it burst. At once she had weaned the baby and gone back to Madame Cecchi with her household money and her money for Christmas. She had not told Gus. Madame Cecchi said her voice was richer now, dramatic — perhaps in the old days she had misjudged. Soon Elizabeth would have to confess to her husband because, if I had any interest at all, she was singing the Bach Christmas oratorio next Sunday: in a local church. They were paying her fifty bucks.

Gilbert came to stand above me, stealing across the room.

"You're home early."

He said: "You've been to the wars."

"It was nothing." Knowing I would not find him falsely sympathetic, I tore the bandage off. For the moment that was painful. He looked tired, dead tired. As he undressed I saw by the closet light that he was seriously burned by the tropical sun.

"No more of these trips," he said and told me how curious it was that like a randy salesman he had followed an attractive Spanish woman right out of a church.

"And I felt so damn old while you were gone," I said and did not sense that was truly an inappropriate reply.

He said: "I've seen my son. Palm Beach. I went there, Maude. He's a limp clergyman, empty. He's affected. I never knew the boy, but I cannot . . ."

He lay beside me silent and stiff, with his courtier's beard. Gentleman. Scholar. Soldier in the name of reason, a humble cause. "I cannot . . ." He could not finish his sentence. My husband is never at a loss for words. It had rained here, I said, filling in. But was not cold. For the first time in years I had not taken the messages off my tape. Then worried on that I had not yet bought Eileen, his secretary, a scarf or purse. Soft as a moth darting, Bert touched my face — not near the eye — to quiet me. And I never said a word about Elizabeth, that it was a miracle, her singing. He took my consoling hand off his scalded flesh and put it down to his hard cock. Some unfinished business. He took my nightgown off. There was hilarity in our coupling and relief.

"The blind and the halt," Bert said, his body on fire, my eye blurred with therapeutic tears. Call it an acrobatic feat.

Waiting for sleep, I asked: "What did she look like?"

"Languid. Streaky blond. He's a delicate youth. Certainly no man of God."

Turning from him, I said that I had extracted pathos from the crowd with my chalazion and that we must have the piano tuned. I listed our Christmas invitations. The slipcovers were badly worn. I did not fully confess that I'd come apart at the seams, exhibited my heart scraped raw, but said that I'd been sentimental about 1954, about New Haven and Frank Dowd, and that the only death that honestly pursued me was the death of that boy, poor Warren jumping in the snow.

"Poor Warren was predictable," he said.

We lay half-listening to the wind on the Hudson, then slept in the bobbing light cast from the trembling streetlamp just below.

GRACE
NOTE

who went briefly to school. Though Jane was sickly and stayed home, she had the brains. It was finished, the peculiar talk about the meaning of those poems. Donna thumped the trash can down the steps toward her car. Roy and the kids had helped her cleaning out. Now the house was sold. This was the last.

She had sold the house: *Colonial, 1790. Original family. 2 fplcs. 4 bdrms. 2-plus acres. Needs work.* And she liked the man who bought it, an orthopedic surgeon with family. They would be weekend people. They loved the wide floorboards and the horsehair poking out of dry plaster where the ceiling was down.

At the dump, Donna Meeker backed up to the pit. The can was heavy with papers. Roy had helped her with the rest. She stood over the void and flung them — pages, line after line, words. That was the end of it.

The Reverend Theodore Lasser looks at his calendar. He is never free. Though he knows the appointed hours for evensong, choir, vestry and AA, he turns the thin blue page of his calendar to see. Each afternoon he hopes to find a blank: reading his appointments he experiences a momentary dip in spirit that might be caused at this time of day by low blood sugar but which he knows to be his daily loss of will. Old Moffit and his wife are tapering off, shamelessly playing bridge and golf, dining out while it lasts. The work of Saint Clement's falls to Theodore Lasser — to Father Lasser, as some call him — who is never free of the rituals and busywork that make his evenings. This night he will sing for his supper, walk

THE RIVER was high. You could see it from the porch where Donna Meeker stood with the trash can. That winter there had been heavy snow. Spring rain. And the river rose halfway up Indian Rock. She and Roy had cleaned the house before Christmas, painted it out white after all the years. Donna knew why she inherited, though she was German and Catholic, only married to a Meeker. Once, when a girl, she had been thrown out of school for something with a boy she did not want to remember. Mattie, who was wild, took her in. That was like Mattie, to reward her for her only sin. Roy, of course, was pleased. The money from the sale of the house. The kids were pleased and said they should give up the farm. She would never live here.

Even with the coat of paint the place was filthy. Mattie was a foul old woman without modern plumbing or a phone. Donna locked up. It was so miserable the yard, so overgrown. All her life it had been an embarrassment — the Le Doux place. One sister writing that poetry to the Meekers' shame. Sex, apparently, and politics. And Mattie — whitewash that. It was finished. The stories were finished about the gin bottles, the Cadillacs, the boyfriends — easy come, easy go. In fact it was Mattie on the water, turn the other cheek and not come back to his bachelor quarters in the rectory until long after midnight, when the Floridian air is chill and cobwebs (which look to him, to a northerner, like frost that will surely kill) threaten his favorite white camellia and the new lemon tree.

Polly is drunk. Ted Lasser can see it in her control, the words she does not slur, the bright look that fixes on the platter of chicken cutlets too long, in her repeated request for the Parker House rolls when one is there uneaten on her bread-and-butter plate. Edwin is sober, always now, allowed one glass of his good claret, but fading fast, worn out from talking too loud, too long: he does not hear others. Two black maids circle the table pouring ice water, checking butter pats. Two women in middle age who came to Polly as Negro servants thirty years ago, living their marriages, births and deaths politely offstage, serving with no change, as far as Ted Lasser can tell, no perceptible change in their attitudes or their demeanor. He would like to snap his napkin at the fat one's ass, get her to sass him with black talk, come to life. His thoughts run petty and mean at Polly's table. He might be twelve or fourteen again, seething with adolescent rage, and this his first dinner with the "idle rich."

The room is harshly lit by a crystal chandelier. The meal is unsalted, soft and damp. Partly doctor's orders and partly arrogance. Polly gets her kitchen staff to cook from an old *Fannie Farmer,* to simulate boarding-school meals — or perhaps it is hotel food — of long ago. All of a piece, this dinner, with Polly and Edwin's Yankee front. They have lived in exile, slummed it in this blown-up hacienda since 1945. Something unspeakable to do with taxes and in summer they must flee to an island off Maine, but the point of reference is always Boston. The canned peas, the neatly darned linen tablecloth, this glaring light on the vanilla ice cream with bottled fudge sauce, Ted Lasser takes to be Polly's version of Boston.

Dinner contains scenes of unguarded passion in which she turns to him and tosses off "the Fogg," "the Symphony," "the Common" to establish further intimacy with the Reverend Mr. Lasser, whose mother lives in Concord and is a Phipps. Brittle connections of family and property have shattered and her Beantown litany of "Fogg," "Common," "Charles," "Yard" is what she has left to pass to him. He is unmerciful. She's drunk. And he has told Polly nicely enough in the clear light of day that his mother lives in Newton, drives mechanically to the classroom and the lab, could live in Keokuk or Boise for all she sees of Boston. But he must be good with Polly and so he makes direct mention of Harvard using the broad Kennedy *a,* and goes on to refer to the Athenaeum, where his stepfather does at least pay dues. He is working toward a Christmas check that should be made out tonight to Saint Clement's.

But Edwin is fading. He no longer talks at the woman sitting next to him, who understands little English. The woman lives next door in a setup like the Alhambra, recently bought from a Swiss banker. Speaking, trying to say so terrible are things in her country, but she hasn't the words and mimes as in a charade played against the clock, anxiously repeating gestures that Ted Lasser takes to be blindfold, handcuffs, key. No, no, she says. The woman looks very rich, but he has no luck with these people. They are Roman Catholics and suspect that most young clergymen are communists at best. The woman makes them understand that her husband is away on business in Milan.

"Just awful," Polly says as though that is another tragedy caused by brutal political factions. She is in control as she rises from the table. "Tell — Señora" — she has forgotten the neighbor's name — "tell her about the fountain."

The fountain is a scam: Father Lasser collects money for the restoration of Saint Clement's fountain. With what he gets out of Polly and Edwin alone he might restore Versailles or the Villa d'Este — well, not really, but the bishop laughed. It is getting somewhat risky, not one crack in the basin is patched. The damn thing is rusted, clogged with grit. He tells the Señora about Saint Clement's fountain. She can advise him on the Spanish tiles. He is wearing down and thinks uncharitably of his boss, the Reverend Mr. Moffit, who should be here for the dirty work but is at a backgammon tournament with his wife. He tells the Señora that as an American he has no eye for Moorish patterns and smiles at her shyly. The woman takes him to be a fool and speaks sharply in Spanish. He cannot understand but feels her full and justifiable contempt.

They drink brandy in a study that captures Beacon Hill. The *Boston Globe,* the *Christian Science Monitor* lie folded so neatly Ted Lasser presumes they are unread. His constant put-downs come to mind as automatic as a tic. Polly is drunk — "Happy New Year. Happy New Year" — blurring this week with the next. Edwin revives. He looks over-the-hill distinguished, a bad copy of Dean Acheson or Anthony Eden set out to wither in the sun. Edwin talks at him. Awful element at The Breakers. Moffit would do well with government bonds. Jews are clever with cheap land. Theodore Lasser draws back as though struck, but he is working hard and makes sure that Edwin sees him in profile, unmistakably Jewish, upsetting and queer. The old man reaches into a drawer for his checkbook: no matter what he believes, he will never be unkind.

Polly comes out with Father Lasser to the door. In her long green dress and pageboy hairdo (silver-gray), with her arm through his, she might be his girl. He puts his hand up to the drying needles of a pine wreath. She breathes excellent brandy on him. "Isn't it a shame," he says to Polly, "that winter in Boston is too severe."

It is early and he drives to Buena Vista, through low shingle-posts, past a flowerbed washed in dramatic light. This entrance has haunted him — a park or cemetery he's seen. Tonight he places it: Buena Vista, the wood-stained sign, odd Japanese lanterns, low bush against rock — the fixtures are identical to those outside a seafood restaurant he has been taken to in Boca Raton.

Now he visits Charley and Rose. It is his single indulgence. Not frivolous, his caring for these people, but not on the calendar. And tonight he finds them in turmoil,

Rose wringing out bath towels, Charley under the kitchen sink.

"Get the wrench," Rose says. She stands laughing in a puddle. Her hands and bare feet are knobbed at the joints with arthritis. Teddy gets the wrench and bales them out of the mess. He replaces a washer: it is so unlikely, marvelous to him like a moment's grace. Then he sits, unsullied, not even damp, with Charley and Rose Morton, who are happy in their flimsy apartment.

"You get what you pay for," Charley says. He is a vivid lean old man, tough as a walnut shell, who writes letters to the *Miami Herald* about what should be done. He has sold his hardware store in Mount Vernon, Ohio, sold the house and come here to bake Rose in the year-round sun. They are surviving her arthritis and to a degree his bone cancer. They are surviving the marriage of their one lovely daughter to a bum.

Rose puts out cuban crackers curled like fat floury magnolia petals. She will try anything. And she takes out a pair of socks she's darned for Teddy, a clumsy job but it's done. They sit with cups of tea. Ted Lasser can never remember what they talk about — neighbors, the news. It is so ordinary, deeply seductive, and when Charley says he is building a Christmas-tree stand, Ted grabs his socks and says that he must go.

In the safety of his car he is aware for the first time that Charley and Rose are not central. Plain people he may be using as ornamentation in his life to embellish a weak theme. They do not need a minister. He should not play at being their son.

About a mile down the ocean road he stops. He can hear the Atlantic but the headlights only get the trunks of palm trees and flat expanse of sand. He rips off the clerical collar, the black dickey, strips to his linen pants. From the back seat he takes a sport shirt, bright red, patterned with birds and still more palms. Then he drives on to what looks like the end of land, but the road turns abruptly, built right out across a swamp. Ahead the cluster of most recent condominiums are attractive at night, like a small city seen from a plane. He drives toward this magic haze, but behind the fresh plantings and lawns, the markets, and another new bank lies a road with scattered bungalows not noticed by developers, perhaps forgotten.

Here a clapboard shack with roof of corrugated tin sits on an undernourished yard. Yet somehow an orange tree grows. Scrub geraniums sprawl around stiff white lilies in the dust. Mosquitoes from the swamp gather in Ted Lasser's headlights as he parks the car. Sasha comes to the screen door. She lives there with Colòn. The television and radio are on, constant noise she does not hear. Now that Teddy is here he switches the music off, just a football game plays on.

It is one room with a kitchen and a can. A towheaded girl named Sally, five or six years old, still plump with baby fat, crayons over photos in a magazine. Sally travels with Colòn. Presumably his daughter, he takes her around with him when he works the docks. Other times the child goes along with Sasha to the beach or grocery store.

Sasha was found in Coconut Grove outside a movie theater. Wasted with that depthless druggy sparkle in her eyes, she was waiting. Ted Lasser remembered her from

Cambridge, then as someone's girl from Berkeley. That her name was Emily before the revolution. He remembered her as beautiful with greasy hair and a fine complexion under the filth. She did not remember where they might have met and said she was waiting at the theater for Sally and Colòn.

Tonight he has brought clothes picked from Saint Clement's jumble sale, mostly dresses for the little girl, rich kids' stuff. Sasha begins to drag them out, one by one — Liberty cotton, linen, velvet with lace — and she titters, a surface laugh that comes out of her often, after years of drugs. Ted Lasser thinks — these are the dresses she wore as a child. The daughter of a wealthy man who owns newspapers in New York, upstate. There is no memory. She holds the clothes to her body as though they will fit and laughs. *"Dower thyself with the present time,"* he says and she laughs. Over a ten-year span she has just slid on a diagonal down the continent from Oakland to the east coast of Florida, where she lives — six months with Ralph Colòn.

Now she has a job distributing French perfume samples in a Palm Beach store. Looking good, she sprays women, only if they respond to her smile. "Try our fragrance," she says. A proficient French accent has stayed with her and she breathes the perfume's name. Laughing, she sprays Ted Lasser now, his delicate ear and sunbleached hair. "Pretty Boy," she says and gets a tough look from Colòn. But Sasha and Ralph are proud of the job Teddy got her and they wonder at the figures on her paycheck, like children with a shell or pretty stone.

At eleven the game is over. Ted Lasser says: "I've got

work for you, Colòn." Two old ladies need wiring in Palm Terrace and he writes down the names. "Act nice."

"I always act nice," says Ralph Colòn. He's a sweet man, handy, bilingual, taciturn. He is not lazy but prefers to drift with Sally up and down the coast. For months now he has been with Sasha in this house. An empty house in Saint Clement's parish. They have curtains, the television and radio. It's home. The child falls asleep watching the news and Colòn carries her to a cot while Sasha sprays the room with ethyl hexapediol. The smell alone is lethal. But the screens are all poked out and each night mosquitoes feed on the sweaty flesh of Sally's tender legs and arms. Sasha dims a light. Ralph tucks the sheet. It is, at that moment, a touching scene.

At a card table they drink beer. Sasha puts out cookies she has made with Sally in the shape of bells and stars, then folds red Christmas napkins, which she hands to Ted Lasser and Colòn.

"Do 'Father,' " she says, tittering. "Do 'Truly Yours in Christ.' "

Sometimes he does that for these friends, gives them part of a sermon or "Having received Thy gifts we pray" or describes the vestments embroidered with gold he will wear on the next possible occasion. It is a way of ministering to them. Colòn does listen to his singsong words in earnest and Sasha keeps on laughing.

"Do the Holy Ghost," she says.

"No —"

"Faggot," she says and laughs. He is beyond her mindless cruelty and taking her hand explains that he is tired. Tonight he will not mock his priestly role. For a long while the Reverend Theodore Lasser sits drinking beer with Sasha (once Emily) and Ralph Colòn. At some point he watches a housefly slowly wipe its legs, swivel its emerald head. The creature seems dazed, perhaps from the insect repellent. He watches the fly walk into his palm, where it draws in useless wings and then moves on.

It is long past midnight when Ted Lasser returns to the rectory in his red shirt with the palms and cockatoos. Old Moffit, wide awake and disapproving, gets out of bed to witness, and sees him sway across the patio. The young priest stumbles back and forth from bush to lemon tree, brushing and brushing at cold cobwebs that will fade with the morning dew.